THE NEW HUNGER

THE NEW HUNGER

AVRA MARGARITI

PART I
THE UNQUIET
QUICKEN FIRST

M Y SISTER IS throwing a party not a week out of Flesh-Eater confinement.

"Enjoying my homecoming?" Evi asks against my ear. She curls around me, serpentine, the way the bassline garrotes my heartbeat.

The way my own meat-hunger sparks from my stomach, starbursting up to my inflamed gums.

It's good to see that months of torture and degradation didn't affect my sister's organizational skills or her taste for glitter, guts, and glamor.

I survey the ballroom, pressed against a wall of the sprawling mansion that houses Evi's feast. It feels like every Eater in the domed city of Kronos is here tonight. The dancing bodies coil sinuous as silk, a thrum of hunger woven through each fiber. Yet the decadence carries a desperate undercurrent. All these young people—the ones who should feel like my people—have been cooped up for too long, detained in Kratos and the rest of the correctional facilities or keeping a low profile to avoid becoming the government's next target.

Most of us Quickened learned this the hard way.

Kaleidoscopic lights cast ever-shifting scenes across the dance floor: meadows of orgiastic flowers pollinating; celestial bodies imploding in stardust and dark matter; red blood cells traversing bodies from within. It all pulsates in time to the wordless, hypnotic music. I wish I could hack the holo-projector into stillness, but I can't ruin Evi's party. Not after everything she's been through these past seven months while I walked away free and undetected.

When you monster and kill your best friend, and your sister takes the blame for you? When she's released from lock-up and asks you to her homecoming party, hosted by her girlfriend and former detainee-leader of Kratos? You swallow your guilt and cowardice and vow to make things right for the Quickened, in and out of confinement.

Two svelte silhouettes detach from the crowd and amble toward Evi hand-in-hand. An Eater/Healer performer couple, I recall from earlier introductions.

The man is tan where the woman is pale; he, of the silver-hued locks to her raven-black buzzcut. One a Healer, the other an Eater: complementary mutations render them the perfect performance duo. The woman—wearing the same horn implants as Evi used to wear before they were stripped from her in Kratos—lunges for my sister's neck. I tense, ready to protect Evi, but she only laughs as the woman retracts her teeth. She plants a kiss against my sister's cheek, not once letting go of her partner's hand.

Evi's smile grows big enough to split her face clean in half. "Nora, it's time. You know what you need to do, don't you?"

"March," I reply. I'm supposed to slip away into the private upper floors during tonight's entertainment. Jonah March—my sister's girlfriend, homecoming benefactor, and former Kratos inmate—is waiting for me to discuss her plans for reformation. I, who for seven months hid at home and waited inertly for my sister's return, was too numb to acknowledge the riots outside my window.

But this is Era 2 now; no more room for hideaways and anesthetization.

When Evi hugs me for luck, she smells like her old orchid perfume, not the facility's misery-sourness that clung to her skin after she came home to me. "Remember: nobody is more dangerous than yourself."

My sister's eyes are starry with mischief. For a moment, I am reminded of the way we used to be: her leading and me following, trusting her every step of the way.

She turns on her heels and climbs the small podium beside the stage, erected amid the ballroom. The performer couple crosses the glisten-bodied dance floor as well. Twin wing stumps protrude from holes cut into the man's dress—statement art implants of clipped wings. I avert my gaze, nostalgia-nauseous for my old body-mod. I had biohacked it myself: a jellyfish feeding on my blood's nutrients, voyaging my body like a bioluminescent tattoo. Its mated pair resided inside Eden: once my best friend, now another name lost among the dead of Era-1 when the Quickening broke out.

The incident gave some of us a taste for human meat and others an ability to regenerate skin and muscle tissue.

I smother the pain clawing behind my breast. About Eden, the subdermal jellyfish I removed to fly under the radar, the memory of my involuntary monstering. I should go, but curiosity stays in my muscles. I have known Evi all my twenty-two years under the dome, yet she's been a stranger for months. I need to know what my sister has prepared for tonight.

The feral susurration of the music dies down, and the dancing, wildling crowd gathers around the stage—a sleek, black-draped structure awaiting its performers like a gaping maw. My sister looks hungry as she surveys the crowd from her podium—so hungry, and I can't even tell in what way.

These days, there are more ways than one to be young, hungry, and out of control.

Evi's voice is huskier than crushed velvet. More lustrous than the space-black of her hair. It resounds across every crevice and cranny of March's mansion through a speech enhancement algorithm. "In the beginning, there was light."

The spotlights turn refulgent on cue so everyone must shield their eyes. Through the gaps between my fingers—like a child playing peek-a-boo with horror-film monsters before our world toppled on its gory axis—the lighting settles. An imitation of candlelit chiaroscuro.

Two forms enter the stage from opposite directions. The man and woman stand facing each other, shedding their white dresses like cicadas molt skins. A lullabied hush overtakes the revelers.

"Spontaneously, the light mutated," Evi's mesmeric voice narrates. "Darkness settled over everything. And when that happens, for the first time in the history of a small, domed, tightly regulated universe—the monsters come out to play."

Both performers pace gracefully, the way of prey and predator. My hairs prickle in their follicles thanks to envy and the need directed at the figures' bared forms. For me, nudity has never equaled attraction. I fall in neither love nor lust to my sister's befuddlement. Yet the performers' bodies batter me breathless: they lack sexual characteristics—primary or secondary—stretching smooth and featureless under the low light. Artists were sometimes known to undergo this procedure as a dedication to their craft. Those indifferent to sex or gender expression did, too. A surgery I'd always craved, outlawed by the time I turned of age. The city officials—fearing a rise in anti-natalism and pro-transhumanism—named such procedures extreme augmentations and passed stricter guidelines for all mods and implants.

The performers circle each other: one second waltzing like peaceful lovers, the other, trapped animals nipping at each other's heels. When one takes a fluid step forward, the other takes a wary step back; when one curls their lips back, the other hisses. String music offers a keening accompaniment to the dancers' brutally vulnerable ebb and flow. The woman crouches in confusion, convulsing as she combats her rising transformation, gnawing on her own arm to soothe a novel starvation that refuses to be slaked.

I look around the audience—the haunted, hungry faces—and know this scene hits too close to home for some—those who fought the Quickening at first, those who failed.

"There was darkness, and there was hunger. And both came on so suddenly, several days into a sunlit and sated creation, catching every creature unawares." Evi's voice is seductive as much as it is mourning.

Someone in the crowd weeps. Their friends and partners comfort them, freeing the crier's bottom lip from self-punishing, sharp teeth. Not everyone hurt another citizen during Era-1 of the Virus, but most came close to it, those first baffling, agonizing days of the Quickening.

This is supposed to be my world, my people. And yet, I feel forever separate from them. Wrapped in the mantle of protection—of privilege—my sister afforded me when she concealed my Eater status from the authorities. I am not exempt from the struggles of the Quickened but isolated from their collective grief and regrouping.

"In the gardens of Arcadia, there was plenty if one knew where to look and how to ask."

The dancers pull apart and collide, over and over, like magnets, molecules, or galaxies subsuming each other until they lock at last in an embrace. So flush with each other, their internal organs must be compressed, corseted. Their muscles shudder, then grow pliant until the fight leaves them altogether. An acceptance of newfound transfiguration. The music grows louder, more urgent. A climax about to come unraveled. Unrepressed.

I shake myself, using the crowd's distraction before denouement to escape the ballroom ambience. I weave toward the DNA-helix staircase at the back. Yet on the landing, I look around. The crowd—glittering, starveling—falls away, and for a second, only my sister remains.

It might be a trick of the light, but Evi looks so desolate, even among her transfixed followers. Her face slackens, devoid of all emotion, yet her voice charms the audience to tears.

Ducking under a red-braided rope, I ascend. The polished marble staircase looks old as history, though Kronos' steel-and-cement lungs have breathed for a single century. Ours is only the second wave of climate-catastrophe domed communities, after the prototype-cities of Gaia and Ouranos had proven a success of self-sufficiency. Nothing in this city is truly old but merely masquerading as such.

The mansion echoes with murmurs of movement and music. My sister's projected voice follows my every footstep. Further down the hall, a vine-blooming wall undulates viridescent. It takes me too long to realize this is no VR illusion. The wallpaper is static, unlike my hunger-born dizziness. If I hadn't wallowed in my sisterly guilt, I would have booked a feeding session with one of my regular Healers before Evi's party.

The next door is private access only. I scan my irises into the spyhole sensor and blink the smarting pain away. The mansion evokes a speakeasy with its revelry and its secrecy. Guests recline on vector and damask upholstery or move languidly around the gilded lounge. They drink from bottomless glasses—Bloody Marys glinting red with something more than tomato juice. On a divan, a group of people move in amorous configurations, their genders impossible to tell apart.

While the lower tiers thrummed with a restless aggregation of energy finally coming unsealed, the air of this room is regal and refined, its occupants assuming relaxed poses and apathetic moues like another prohibition-era reenactment. The only constant is the hunger.

Not just for flesh, either. These are the youth deemed unquiet even before they Quickened. The ones advocating for somatic augmentations and sexual autonomy. The mayor called us a cancer to the city long before the Virus spontaneously mutated us.

As the city's favorite propaganda goes, the unquiet Quicken first.

Evi's secondhand dress makes me feel more like a creature than a girl. I stand in the middle of the lounge, ignored by the guests in their fineries. A multidimensional holograph displays the ballroom performance from all angles, Evi's voice slinking through. Omnipresent.

"Nature's gifts are most plentiful. If there is a new hunger, there too shall be a new satiety."

Still locked in a sexless, smooth-skinned embrace, their flesh nearly fused into a singularity, the man bares his throat at the woman. My mouth throbs like an open wound, the sweet memory-scent of meat overwhelming. Like caramel and charred fat and the secrets exchanged in dreams.

It's different now, the hunger. We feed often, and only from sanctioned, compensated individuals. It is a creature capable of control, even as it stabs at our guts and gums. Unlike Era-1 of the Virus, when everything was red, red and ravening. Our minds watched, immobilized in liquid terror, as our bodies devoured those close to us or died of newborn cellular autophagy.

Onstage, the woman feeds on her partner's proffered body parts. The light haloes them; it anoints the willing spill of blood. The guests in the lounge erupt into applause, and, on cue, a side door opens. People wearing faux-silk scarves of red enter the room one by one.

The Crimson Ribbons are decked out in beautiful suits and dresses. Black, to hide the stains of gore. They weave with cygnine grace between the lounging partygoers, stretching their pomegranate-swathed necks. When an Eater beckons, the Crimson Ribbon follows. They relinquish their flesh to the altar of our hunger in exchange for creds transferred to their accounts, clout among March's crowd, and the endorphin-high of regeneration. Even, perhaps, for the knowledge that, by feeding us, the Crimson Ribbons are rebelling against Kronos' authority.

Yet, for all that this party hails itself as inclusive—revolutionary—no Healer has been invited besides the hired Crimson Ribbons working the lounge. Though most Healers weren't hounded and imprisoned like the Eaters were post-Quickening, domed Kronos didn't let any of its children escape their transformations unscathed. The city is still trying tooth and nail to document and control its Healers—another facet of the so-called unquiet youth.

I avert my eyes from the symbiotes entwined mid-feeding. My sister always called me hypervigilant—another word for killjoy—but I cannot conjure up the vulnerability required for a public feeding. There are no windows here to offer a view into the city: skyscraper spires nearly tall enough to pierce the dome, stars obfuscated by smog and glass. No fresh air to relieve this meat-haze asphyxiation as my needlepoint teeth bloody my hungry tongue.

I focus on my sister's amplified voice; the cadence as familiar as her messianic words are foreign. Just where the hell is March? Evi said our host would know when I entered the private lounge. Her girlfriend would come and collect me.

"I know you," drifts a voice from the velvet chaise longue.

My heart catches burr-like in my chest. But it's not March, only an Eater not much older than my twenty-two years under the dome. He hangs languid and drunk off the back of the chaise, his eyes—modified a neon green of slitted pupils and nictitating membranes—never once leaving mine. A Crimson Ribbon perches beside him. The fresh wound on her upper arm—glistening meat-pink with a coquettish flash of white bone—clashes with her spiky purple hair.

"I know you," Cat-Eyes drawls. "Evi's snotty little sister. You've got nerve coming here."

"I'm sorry?" A powdery-dry taste suffuses my mouth. My sister's voice floats from the holo-projection, but she's not here to tell me what to do. And March, still nowhere to be found.

"You think you're so much better than the rest of us? Letting her take the fall for you?"

I do not stumble back at his acid-laced words, but only just.

"I did things. So did Evi. Taking the blame for one less attack wouldn't have changed the outcome," I try to convince him, or myself. I remember the blood staining my hands and the meat clogging my mouth. How Evi found me cradling my best friend's limp body, how she painted her own hands red with the lifeforce I'd stolen, how she tricked Kronos' authorities into taking my place.

How I let her.

My marrow feels leaden like it will wear a hole through the flooring, send me hurtling down among the dancers. I want this encounter to end, but Cat-Eyes is fevering with a hunger for justice, and I do not entirely begrudge him.

"You don't know what happened inside those facilities, Evi's sister. I was there. I may report you, so you'd experience it firsthand. An unregistered Eater. I wouldn't say no to the reward money, either."

Cat-Eyes' pretty mouth bites out every word, smeared with lipstick and ruby blood. His purple-haired companion—skin already knitting back together—tries to pull him in for a post-feeding cuddle, but his eyes are adamantly trained on me, predator-still.

In response, the nacreous nubs of my teeth elongate from my gums. My mouth tastes like the copper wires I forage for my micro-robotics experimentations. Cat-Eyes' body, too, coils wire-tight. I can't hide in Evi's shadow for once and let her do the dirty work for me.

A door opens to my right before either of us does something we regret. A lilting alto says, "Nora, I've been expecting you."

Jonah March wears a charcoal three-piece suit with

a subtle rose relief, dapper like a relic from another century. She's tall and lithe, her severe features carrying a composure beyond her twenty-six years. At once a young, tortured visionary, and an old soul commanding everyone's respect.

I expected nothing less of the object of Evi's affections.

Cat-Eyes hisses yet backs down under Jonah March's level gaze. After all, this is her mansion, her party, despite letting my sister—her star-crossed Kratos lover—do with it as she pleases.

I glance at the holo-screen of Evi's performance one final time. Then, I let March beckon me inside her office, where everything is wainscoting, leather, marble, and brocade. Grecian and Rococo details weave through the art deco—the 23rd century is known for mixing its metaphors and aesthetics. The only modern juxtaposition lies in March's tattoo modification: a snake opening and closing its jaw. I wonder if the ink is venomous to the touch.

"What did you think of the performance?" March's smooth voice inquires. She sits behind her polished-wood desk while I slide in a wingback chair across from her. A pomegranate still life hangs behind her, arils glistening red as blood vessels. The painting is dated before the birth of Kronos—when the still-domeless city was only known as Athens. Not a replica, then; March must own more money and power than I thought. Importing all these old-world relics into the city of Kronos—with its aspiring self-sufficiency and strictly controlled energy resources—comes with hefty fees deposited into the mayor's pockets.

I chew the coppery inside of my cheek. March's study is soundproof, but I swear my sister narrates her neo-creation myth inside my head. "Good for entertaining a crowd," I say. "But we both know divine gifts and nature's bounties are not how the Virus happened."

March smiles wryly. We're both thinking about it—the new hunger and the new punishment.

City officials called it a spontaneous gene-mutating virus once they stopped blaming body mods and debauchery. It affected a subset of the under-twenty-five population—the ones without a fully matured frontal lobe was the theory. Made us subsist solely on human flesh or die with a meat-hunger on our lips. Those who managed to control their first feeding were put on surveillance databases and under home arrest. And those who acted in the slightest violence—succumbing to the fear of a rapidly transforming body—were carted off to the correctional facilities. Their rights were violated, and their bodies were experimented on in search of a cure for the newer generation—we've all seen the leaked Era-1 footage of the cluster cities named a humanitarian crisis.

The leather straps constrict all movement, the needles sticking out of exposed veins.

And then, there are people like me. Changed by the Quickening but living a clandestine existence. All thanks to my sister's sacrifice.

"Evi said you were smart." March steeples long fingers adorned with skull rings. The snake weaves between her knuckles as if to swallow the gemmed skulls, crush them like eggshells between its throat. "We need people like you if we are to make a change in Kronos."

Evi met Jonah March in Kratos, one of Kronos's worst correctional facilities. An early success case of contained monstering, March was among the first to get out. Hungry not just for meat but for revolution. This is the cause Evi wants me to join: a movement to stop the vilification of the Eaters and the disparagement of the Healers, who volunteer their flesh to keep us alive.

Despite the room's optimal temperature, a chill needles my spine. "What can I do for your cause, exactly?" I have to remind myself that I am here for Evi but also for myself.

March sizes me up. When her lips part in a smile, they show off her teeth: once white and straight; then lengthened by the Virus; finally, filed to bluntness in the facility. They are the only imperfect thing about her.

"You are unregistered, unlike every other Eater in

this party. You can move through Kronos without raising suspicions or being questioned by the authorities."

It feels like a blow to the diaphragm, though it's true. No Quickened status blemishes my ID wrist-patch. Nothing to trigger the checkpoints around the city the way my sister does whenever she enters any building, vulnerable to stares and judgment. To violence, too. The news, once full of tributes to the citizens hurt by the Eaters' unfettered first feeding, now reports vigilante attacks against the Quickened. Yet every story carries a subtext of what did you expect, showing your faces around the city?

"Nora," March says—a tone aiming for kindness.

I shake off my trance. "Sorry. You were saying?"

"Thanks to Evi's quick thinking, you are completely off-grid. You can be my eyes and ears—an extension of myself to help our cause. And your hacking skills…" March inclines her head—a show of admiration as constrained in emotion and economical in movement as everything about her. "I heard you have a centipede. Nora's copperwire plaything, your sister called it. Small, sleek, subtle mechanism that can perform in-person data collection undetected."

Gods above, Evi and her loose lips. My hand travels to my dress pocket, but the copperwire centipede I've been fiddling with for years is safely stored back home.

What March wants is espionage. My aid in a post-Era-2 redefinition of the ties between Eaters, Healers, and the non-Quickened. We had no say in the previous laws, too disjointed during Era-1 to organize; Healers and Eaters too dispirited to realize that ours are sibling causes, much like our metamorphoses are complementary. But Era-2 is only a name the city uses to lull itself, post-apocalypse; to say, look, we unlocked some of the prisons and laboratories, we let the Crimson Ribbons handle your flesh-feedings. So what more do the unquiet youth want from us?

"Will it be dangerous?" I sound like a little kid again, nightmare-ridden and sleeping in my sister's bed while our parents stayed out all night, squeezing dry Kronos' Golden Twenties.

"Yes," says March, with no frills or flair. "But keeping the Quickened from cowering in the shadows until the city crumbles to dust is a cause you will find worthy in time."

Something inside me protests her prediction. "Cat-Eyes was right, you know. I'm a coward. I devoured my best friend and let Evi face what should have been my consequences."

Eden... They were more than just a best friend, though there was nothing just—nothing lesser—about what we shared. But how do I explain to March the long sleepovers of unspoken secrets, copperwire trinkets, ghost stories? The crying sessions, cutting sessions—kissing sessions. The wishing to be each other's everything even when Eden loved me in every way the word love could apply, and I was too ace and aro to be in love, but still, I fucked them tender with our favorite strap, still, I promised to grow old with them in a city far from all-devouring Kronos. But what I did instead was dig my eyeteeth into Eden's flesh and—

My gums ache. My lips taste saltier than the shores of Okeanos under its sunbaked solar dome, the singular time I visited another cluster-city as a child. Silently, March hands me an amber drink from a crystal decanter as I wipe away the errant tears. I chug the whiskey although the flavor has dulled to a faint afterburn since I Quickened. No food, drink, or drug tastes like much or holds any nutritional value. To sate oneself and survive, only human meat will do. Even the scientists' stem-cell 3D-printed meat did nothing to quench our hunger as they shoved it down our restrained throats.

March says, "I kept your sister safer than most during confinement. I was on my best behavior and got out early, built new connections in Kronos, and got Evi released not long after."

She kept Evi safe, and I didn't, is the implication.

"I'll consider your offer," I say through a dough-thick tongue choking my airways.

My decision should have been an easy one, based on kinship with my fellow Eaters, allyship with the Healers and our interconnected struggles. Yet I still feel like a specter, separate from it all. I didn't see community when I roamed March's mansion. I saw pangs of hunger, and I saw hunger, sated. I saw everyone having a damn good time without acknowledging this past mad year. The post-Quickening mass memorials and the scandals of the correctional facilities. The major tragedy of the good citizens of Kronos and the minor suffering of the Quickened—Kronos' disgraced children.

I stand up to leave as quick as my dignity allows.

"Fine by me," comes March's easy answer. "Oh, and Nora?"

I hover awkwardly, jittery in March's antiques-filled office. It's hard to picture her in any other setting, clad in anything but her luxurious suit. The gray cement walls of Kratos' holding cells; the dirty rags they called a uniform. I've seen the videos posted all over cyberspace, although Evi has kept tight-lipped about it all.

"You might want to take the side exit," March offers—so patient it feels pitying. "Avoid your little friend out there."

I think about Cat-Eyes fevering for a fight, the Crimson Ribbons donating meat in the lounge, under my sister's hypnotic narration, and the near-tangible sting of my hunger.

"Thanks," I mutter, ducking behind a floral folding

screen next to an ornate free-standing mirror. All vintage, all costing a not-so-small fortune by Kronos' standards—ours has never been the richest of the domed cluster-cities.

The screen conceals the doorway of a utility corridor. I exit March's office and follow the cramped tunnel, shining bioluminescent at intervals and smelling like mold and aging wine. It turns my empty stomach on each inhale. The mansion is old. Old money. I climb down a crepuscular stairway parallel to the ballroom's drumbeating walls, then finally reach the kitchen, where I can slip out the back door unobserved.

Except, when the air flow cleanses, freed of the birth-canal-clutch of the utility corridor, I nearly collide with someone entering through the kitchen access. Someone with features as familiar as the Healer's ribbon flashing red around their throat. Someone I unwittingly attacked when the hunger first struck me, leaving my best friend a crumpled husk on my bedroom floor.

"Eden," I whisper, like breath is a luxury I cannot afford. "You can't be here."

What I mean to say is: You're dead. I killed you.

Eden studies me with an unreadable expression on their once-soft face. My best friend. My lover. My ghost with the crimson ribbon like a slit throat.

"Gods," Eden utters in the same low voice I

remember, its euphony marred by a new whetted edge. I lean against the counter to balance myself. "Jonah was right. You really came."

Staggering footsteps and peals of laughter approach through the kitchen's main entrance. It sounds like the pre-programmed tripping of a Psychopomp injection—Kronos' drug du jour. Reaching through my stupor, Eden leads me by the elbow out into the back garden. We stand on a darkened flowerbed while strains of syncopated revelry pulsate from within the mansion. Yet out here, it feels like we are the only ones in the world, me and my ghost.

Me and my guilt.

"I knew Evi would be here partying her trauma away. But you—came at last to see your handiwork for yourself?"

Eden unwinds the scarf from around their neck. I stumble back at the palimpsest patterns of my own teeth marks between their neck and shoulder. I gape at the best friend I mutilated and mourned. In the moonlight, the ribbon glows silver. But I know its true color, and what it symbolizes.

"You're a Healer?" Not only that but a Crimson Ribbon, too.

When the Quickening first erupted, and the riots, and the fires that burned through Kronos' blood-smeared streets for days, we didn't know there was a healing mutation too, counterbalancing and supplementing our hunger. We didn't know there could be meat given without pain. There was no time. It felt like death, that hunger. Hurt down to each molecule, set our marrows aflame. Like if I didn't eat right then I would turn into a desiccated vessel.

Like Eden was, after I dropped their body in the dissolution of my meat-haze.

I was catatonic with horror when Evi found me, nuzzling a torn-off gobbet of Eden to my cheek like a childhood toy. My sister said she'd take care of it. Scrubbed me clean and ordered me to hack the car's AI so no one would trace my coordinates. Go as far away as I could and not come back without her say so.

I drove past burning dumpsters and street fights— Quickened against unQuickened; then the retaliation: adult turning against adolescent. At last, the vacant countryside beyond Kronos' dome came into view, distorted through glass and air pollution. Far above, the smothered stars resembled fake little baubles like everything else in the city. I curled up in the driverless car and cried for the best friend I had vowed to protect from the world but failed to save from myself.

When I came back, Evi had been dragged off to Kratos and Eden's body was missing. Nothing left but to stay all alone in that empty apartment, me and my double-edged guilt.

My world spins with dissonant thought fragments. Eden is here. My sister must be looking for me. It was stupid of me not to feed earlier because seeing my teeth indentations on Eden's skin makes my heart throb with need and nausea.

"Eden, please. Let me go now but come find me afterward. Like we used to. I'll explain."

Eden stares at me, their unraveled ribbon clutched in one fist like a string of guts undulating in the breeze. Like my own heart flensed and flayed to ribbons.

At last, they nod. "Later, then. Hope you find a good excuse by then."

Eden disappears inside the kitchen and through the utility corridor—into March's office? Eden is a Crimson Ribbon now, working to slake our meat-hunger with their regenerating flesh. I picture March feeding. Slotting her teeth over the marks I left on Eden's body when the end of the world came down upon us, voracious and ungovernable.

In the moon's silver-breathed light, I lean against a hedgerow and vomit red, red juice.

EVI STUMBLES OUT of March's mansion, drunk and laughing like the grind of broken glass. Her giggles are laced with the desperation of someone who spent her twenty-sixth birthday in slapdash confinement, poked by hypodermic needles and electric prods like a wild beast.

All because of me and this new hunger the universe bequeathed to us both.

March has commandeered a self-driving cab to take Evi and me back to our empty apartment. The windows are black-tinted, and the leather seats are warm. I guide my sister inside, careful to tuck her stained, torn dress around her as the automatic door closes. Right away, the mansion's disco heartbeat vanishes. Yet Evi's homecoming is far from over.

Evi, Jonah March, and I have so much work to do. And now Eden, too.

Did Evi know the best friend I hurt in my monstering was alive and under March's patronage? Is that why she brought me to this party—what she and March both planned to convince me of their suicidal scheme?

We're a little bit sick, Evi and I. We use and manipulate people. I have always denied it, but it's true. Something to do with our half-feral upbringing, neglect, and codependence. Two apples rotting together, sister to sister, core to core.

"Fine," I bite out. "Tell March I said yes."

Evi slips an uncoordinated arm around me. The sour sweat of her hair wafts up to my nose, perfumed with a residue of meat. Boneless, she slumps down the backseat while we hurtle through the streets of Kronos. Outside our cab, parties rave all over town in celebration of newly lifted curfews. Already, things are changing again. I crack the windows open and smell rage cutting through the revelry; my generation's suppressed energy is just beginning to overflow.

I can't do this, Evi. Please don't make me be the adult between us.

Yet Evi has already fulfilled her sentence. The only sentence I carried was my guilt.

"Nora," my sister croons as she falls asleep on my lap. "I'm so glad I'm home."

MY HEAD FEELS too light, my body too heavy. Half of me will float up to the city's solar dome while the rest sinks to some chthonic realm. I push my fingers against the ache in my jaw, holding them fast against the thrum of hunger until we're home. Too bad I can't do the same with my heart—press down against the atriums and ventricles until it stops trying to shake me apart to the tune of Eden's name.

I half-run to our elevator, zooming past dozens of skyscraper apartments; then to our front door, where I bark a voice command to unlock. I'm so hungry, it reminds me of the passing-out game, and that time in high school I went too close to the dark place in my head. The caterpillar-fuzziness had taken so long to dissolve.

Intoxicated, Evi slips straight into her bedroom. I kept it untouched in her absence, a mausoleum to my sister's image. I linger, torn between preparing our parents' old bedroom for my emergency feeding session and ensuring my sister is alright. Tucking her in, bringing a basin by her bedside in case she needs to purge all that alcohol during the night.

I do not check on Evi. The thought of my sister potentially keeping Eden from me sours my caring streak and codependence. Eden.... I need to feed soon if they are to visit later, sneaking into the balcony garden like we used to at all hours of the night when we were in school.

While I wait, I check on our apartment's altar. The habit is born of superstition—half-hearted pantheism to keep the city's dome from falling on our heads. Steel, glass, and cement are the only gods and giants my people know how to worship. I light a candle among the twenty-six waxen stubs. One cluster for Gaia and Ouranos, prototype progenitors of all domed cities. Then two dozen more: twelve candles for the Titans, first-wave cluster-cities saving a moribund world from climate catastrophes and energy depletion. The last twelve candles represent the second wave: Olympian cities of cutting-edge technology we can never access. Not with our own shabby city lowering its dome firmly to the ground.

Post-Quickening, no one is leaving Kronos, the city that devours its young.

The apartment's overhead lights flash a triple-blink pattern, and I go to the door to greet tonight's Healers hired through the Synergy app. Before Evi's homecoming, I had to get creative, keeping feeding sessions discreet. The only thing that had saved me from the authorities banging on my door was that so many neighboring apartments were left empty in the wake of the Quickening. Anyone who could have turned an unregistered Eater in had moved houses or worse.

My only regulars available tonight were the Andreadi twins: nineteen years old under the dome, vintage leather-clad, with old-school static tattoos and puffy clouds of pale hair. During the Quickening, the twins found their little brother cowering and near-starving in his room, and they did not hesitate before offering their flesh to ease his pain. They are Crimson Ribbons now, working to aid the community, grateful they could keep their little brother alive.

"You poor thing," Anna greets me while Maria brushes past me into the kitchen to prepare tonight's aftercare supplies. As a safety precaution, healers usually work in pairs, though I suspect the twins simply enjoy each other's company. "You must be famished."

"Yeah, I…" I trail off, swaying on the spot. "Evi ate at the party, so it's just me tonight."

Taking pity on me, Anna leads me into the bedroom, her calloused hand steady in mine. Though she is younger than me, I follow her like a little lost kid. She is seated on the double bed and reveals a low-cut tank top under her cardigan.

"Left shoulder blade tonight, please," Anna encourages, and I nod mutely, teeth elongated with painful relief.

This is unlike the first feeding when resisting the song of the Quickening felt like death, slow and agonizing. I can control my hunger, even if it punishes me. Looking at Anna one final time for permission, I chomp down on her bare shoulder, tearing a good chunk of meat to crunch between my teeth.

The taste is butter-rich and gravy-savory. A meal after starving yourself, a favorite childhood recipe you can never truly recreate. When our minds connect during the act's crescendo, I can hear Anna's thoughts: need to pick up milk from the auto-vendor/is my sister getting enough sleep/what if one day the city gorges itself on us all? Maria, on the other hand, often dreams of birds of paradise and stained glass shattering. Of retirement, she and her sister running away to join the infamous underground circus of Rhea, the floating libraries of Coeus, or one of Hyperion's farming communes.

"Does it hurt?" I asked the twins the first time I

hired them in Synergy's encrypted chatrooms, paying extra for them to keep my Eater status a secret. I tried to be gentle—as gentle as one can be with someone else's flesh between their teeth.

"It's only a sting at first," the twins had reassured me. "Then the regeneration endorphins kick in. It feels good afterward, like cold cream on a sunburn."

I swallow the lingering meat fullness, and it slides wet down my throat. It never gets any easier; this guilt associated with my first feeding, although I know it was beyond my newly mutated body's control. Except Eden is alive. It feels like something I hallucinated during the party amid variegated smoke, bass, and algorithmic strobe lights.

Feasts like tonight's party are an outlier. Most of my new kin only eat twice a week, though Evi needed to feed daily after her release from Kratos. Me, I can go up to ten days without a bite. Evi would say this is because I have always run cold. Like an old fable's vampire, she would say, not a drop of warm blood in me, even as our generation's blood bubbled and boiled.

I wipe my mouth clean and hand Anna some healing-accelerant ointment. I hold a mirror aloft as she applies a self-adhesive, nanite gauze—calmly, if a bit stupefied—over the gap of missing meat, a peek of fibrous sinew in her shoulder already beginning to string itself back together. I clean the rest of the spill with an antibacterial towel.

Anna and I cuddle for our usual aftercare while her twin prepares tea and toast in the kitchen. She sighs contently as the endorphin-rich regeneration manifests; the meat I just consumed soothes the burn of my own system, snuffing out the pain. Healers and Eaters, irrevocably interrelated.

"There's talk of a revolution." Anna's feeding-drunk whisper ruffles my hair, the raven strands tickling my neck. "You seem to be smelling of it, love."

"It was just a party," I say, though the words taste empty, leaving crevices for the truth to burrow.

"We're in the Era-1 aftermath, Nora. Party, protest—can you really tell them apart?"

I think about March's mansion. How perhaps the endless, dazzling decadence is a front. A hub for the young and the angry: once captured, tormented, degraded, and now intoxicated with their newfound freedom. A new solidarity is built among Kronos' abandoned children as their pent-up energy is channeled into revelry—revolution.

Maria enters the room with a tray of tea and calorie-dense snacks to assist Anna's regeneration. "There's a pretty thing out on the balcony waiting for you."

I scrambled upright, thinking: Eden. They were real. They are here.

When I glance guiltily at a drowsy-looking Anna, she laughs only. "Go on. Maria and I have things under control here."

I will remember to upload more credits to the twins' balance, although it will cost me later.

The back balcony garden has overgrown in the absence of a grooming bot's touch, with grass nearly swallowing the delivery drones' drop-off zone. The whole apartment our parents abandoned during their indefinite vacation has succumbed to neglect during Evi's term in the correctional facility and my own months-long depressive spell.

And in the middle of that wild grass—one of the few small, green oases allotted to Kronos' residents—Eden stands like a statue surveying the city. A nymph, all pale under the silvered night sky but for the crimson ribbon around their throat.

"Hey," I say, quiet so as not to send them a-skitter like the small mammal they sometimes were in the before times. They would run away from their foster home and burrow under my bedcovers at the oddest hours. When I clutched them to my body and refused to give them back.

Eden doesn't turn back to face me, not right away. "You wanted to talk, so talk."

Then they swivel around, and for a resonant, unreasonable second, I love them, and I hate them because they're wearing a beaten-puppy look, and I want to scream, How dare you act like a dog when everyone around you has turned into wolves?

I rein myself in because this is Eden. The one who stuck by me all throughout high school, when I was angry enough to hack and break everything cybernetic or material, when my parents were never around, and Evi and I had to fend for ourselves, when I castigated myself for failing to fall in love. Everyone around me became enamored with the idea of romance. And Eden—fledgling transfem dyke dressed in fading bruises and a sibling's hands-me-down—saw me, from skin to marrow.

I look at them now: eyes too dark for their wan complexion, rust-brown curls falling ragged around their face. Gaunt, when once they were plump despite our peers' manifold diet-drug fads. I can't tear my eyes away from the scars I bequeathed the neck I had so often kissed.

"I thought you were dead," I say, my voice fault-lined down the middle. "I would have looked for you if I'd known. You were fucking dead, and I was the one who killed you."

I want to say I'm sorry, but I can't. Sorry is not a word my sister or I ever learned how to speak. When Eden lived with us after graduation, they apologized for every little thing, a habit beaten into them from children's homes to foster houses. Yet Eden, far from my shadow, built themself a spine of steel in the apocalypse, while my own backbone deliquesced away from the shade Evi cast. What a mess we've made, the three of us.

"I know," Eden enunciates with an eerie calm. "I was there."

"Can you tell me?" I plead. "What happened?"

I crave absolution, yet I will not ask for it. I'm not sure Eden can grant it, either. The wound is too raw between us, and the scars are unfading.

"I remember the pain. Closed my eyes just to make it stop. The scars... even we Healers aren't immortal, you know. We can give what is needed and no more than that. Too much too fast, and the wounded flesh cannot regenerate. It turns to scar tissue instead." Eden smiles wryly. "Even a Healer couldn't come out of a first feeding like ours unscathed."

I, too, close my eyes, though I have no right to this pain.

"Were you alone?" I imagine them bleeding out on my bedroom's cream carpet with no one to hold their hand. Soothe their fear.

"Your sister was there when I woke up... You weren't."

Evi. Of course, she never bothered to mention anything to me. Has my sister been punishing me for letting her take my place in the correctional facility? Is that why she kept Eden's Healer status a secret?

"So you're a live-in at March's mansion now?" My words come out sharper than I intended: jagged glass I cannot dull into sea glass.

Eden's expression calcifies. "You sound like them. The ones who judge us Crimson Ribbons. Call us sick and debased for doing what we do. But everyone must do their part at the end of the world and beyond."

There's bite in their last words—an accusation. Everyone is regrouping and rebuilding after the disaster of the Quickening blindsided us—everyone except for me.

"You're right," I exhale. "Without the Crimson Ribbons, we would grow starved and feral." Would end up back in the facilities, crunched between Kronos' teeth for good. "I was only wondering how you ended up with March."

Eden sighs, considering their next words—if I'm ready to hear them. "March has gathered every stray in the city in the three months since her release from Kratos. Before that, I worked as a Ribbon here and there. Some of my regulars let me crash at their place if we were doing repeat feedings."

My heart constricts. The city secures no dwellings for its orphans past their eighteenth year under the dome. Until the Quickening, this apartment my parents abandoned had been Eden's home as much as my and Evi's.

"I agreed to March's plan." I rush past every craven, guilt-wracked thing clamoring in my throat. "And Evi is March's girlfriend. This means you and I'll see more of each other around the mansion. So can we just...."

Reconcile? Forget what happened between us? My words hang suspended in the nocturnal air, among the drone of cicadas and cleaning bots picking up the day's rubbish from the street far below.

Suddenly, like a droid with a dying battery, Eden drops to the untended grass, uncaring how their sundress stains in verdigris-like patterns.

I sit nearby, cautious of my movements and the space my limbs occupy. Eden does nothing to lessen our distance, but they don't flinch away from me, either.

And we both understand that the world we once navigated together no longer exists. Someone shot a bullet through the world, and this, here, is the exit wound. We cling to its crimped, hemorrhaging edges, trying our damnedest to survive.

I rip out blades of grass and wrap them like tourniquets around my fingers. Traces of gore linger from my earlier feeding, grimed under my fingernails. Burning hot, I rake my fingers through the makeshift garden's thin topsoil, hoping the dirt replaces the blood.

I could reach my hand out to Eden through the wild grass, but I don't.

Silence stretches viscid in time to the wheeling of heavenly bodies. It sometimes feels like Kronos has more skyscrapers than stars. Humans will soon try to build new cities in the sky—not clusters, but constellations of them—because we have already fucked up the one little, green-blue thing that was ours. The cluster-cities of Titans and Olympians cannot protect us forever. Nothing remains impenetrable, not even the domes once sold as a miracle solution to filter polluted air and ultraviolet rays, gather solar power, and inspire unity among their citizens. What a joke our progenitors played on us.

Even as we face the city, I watch Eden from the corner of my eye, and they watch me in return. Like Evi after Kratos, my best friend has become a hungry, haunted specter whose thoughts I can no longer intuit.

Eventually, they speak again. "I should head back. Someone might need me at the mansion. Seeking you out tonight was an impulse."

When they prepare to leave the garden, I call their name out in shameful fragility. I helped them choose that beautiful name when we were in high school, and their old one became an ill-fitting epidermis.

They turn around, starlit and expectant, but, in the end, I cannot say it. Their shoulders slump; Eden hugs themself against a sudden chill.

"See you in the revolution, then."

And they're gone, and only the dark remains.

WHY DIDN'T YOU tell me about Eden? I practice asking my sister while I hover behind her dressing-room mirror.

How March managed to secure Evi this talk-show slot, on one of Kronos' cluster-wide broadcasts, is beyond my imagination. Most likely strong generational connections and a hefty creds transference.

A makeup artist perches on a stool beside Evi, her arm trembling as it holds a brush of real-time flaw-concealing powder midair.

"She doesn't bite," I snap, regretting it immediately as the makeup artist—young, unQuickened—nearly levitates out of her skin in alarm.

I wonder if this girl thinks herself morally superior to Evi and me, just because she was spared from monstering by unknown factors. It's a belief clinging like black mold around the city, that those who didn't Quicken into Eaters or Healers were the good kids, the prudent, rule-abiding youth destined for greatness.

"It's alright, my sister can finish my makeup for me," Evi says, smiling saccharine.

Moth-antennae-mods twitching, the makeup girl scurries away. My sister and I are left alone in the dressing room, too bright and cramped for the things left unsaid between us. With a flick of her wristband, Evi expands her holo-screen, projecting her talk-show notes across the mirror. As I dab self-blending blush across her face, I peek at her notes. Words emerge like, mind games, isolation, starved to near-madness. That's the story angle, then. Evi as Kronos' sweet martyr, stoic survivor of steel-fisted Kratos. Not a lie, but a defanged truth.

Why won't you talk to me about the facilities, but you're ready to tell the whole world? I want to ask.

"Why—" I begin, not knowing if it's Eden's or Kratos' name about to breach the threshold of my teeth.

"Nora," Evi interrupts. She sounds placid enough. Yet behind the brown eyes we share smolders a semblance of desperation. "You're glad to have me back after all this time, aren't you?"

I sputter. "Of course. Why do you even have to ask?"

"Then you'll support me through this. As my sister, you have to."

Evi is stalling, avoiding all my questions as she has for days. Her eyes have oscillated between a faraway glassiness and a calculating edge. Is she scared now? I saw her popping Tran-Q pills in the driverless car March sent for us earlier. My sister is about to walk into the belly of the beast, where the unQuickened host will interrogate her, faking compassion at her story while poking around for plot holes and weak points to exploit for views.

This is the role Evi is called to play in March's revolution. Exposing the festering wounds of the facilities; normalizing the existence of the Quickened throughout Kronos, so that its unmutated citizens—the only ones still enfranchised—do not vote for even more austere measures against us in the upcoming elections.

I still don't know my part in all this. But if it's to involve my data-copying centipede, my assignment won't be as aboveground and sanitized as Evi's media campaign.

"We're ready to go in five," a fidgety tech informs us from outside the dressing room.

Sighing, I mic up Evi by myself, cringing at the outdated equipment. We look so alike in the mirror, my sister and I. Black hair, olive skin, brown eyes. Yet I can't help feeling like a fracture has split the convergence of our reflection.

Evi pats my hand. "Don't look so moody. Today's an important day for all of us."

Ever since my sister came back, I have wanted to say a million things, but the words always die strangled in my throat.

I shuffle toward the wings while my sister strides into the talk-show's set. Compact camera bots and their handlers rush about doing prep-work. My sister sits quiet and composed on the set's faux leather couch, while crew members keep their distance, as if the cell-mutating Virus might crawl out of Evi's mouth and into theirs. Never mind that the Quickening had never been contagious or affected anyone older than twenty-five years under the dome. Even Axiom, the talk-show's hostess, wears a full-bodied robe over her genetically altered slimness, as if any exposed strip of skin might trigger my sister's hunger.

Then, there is Evi, smiling serenely at anyone that dashes by, stoic in her sensible pantsuit and tight ponytail. Her new mod of choice is a subtle one: a mother-of-pearl cutaneous shimmer, activated with every infinitesimal twitch of muscle.

Damn, but I miss my subcutaneous jellyfish, the tentacles that bombinated in tempo with my pulse. Girlhood has always felt to me like a foreign body; a speck of dust scratching my cornea. Yet the type of Good Girl I'm pretending to be would never wear such a disrespectable mod. Would never monster during Era-1 of the Virus, either.

While I wait half-hidden in the wing, I flick open my holo-tab and hunch over the self-scrolling feed. Once upon a time, I would claw at my scalp until it bled in compulsive crimson rivulets. Now, my nervous tic has transmogrified into checking the news: the rocketing Quickened suicide rates; the most recent attacks from either end of the city-wide divide; the story of another illicit meat market, busted. I search the voting-poll predictions to see Mayor Pappas is still in the lead, him and his 'Normality & Naturality' campaign.

Then, bypassing conscious thought, I visit Eden's old TabMe account. The last photo update was seven and a half months ago—mere days before the Quickening. As if they really are dead, their online tracks gone cold. I'd spent hours staring at this photo while locked in my empty apartment. It shows the two of us together, cheek-to-cheek. Our smiles are nothing like the wry flicker of lips that Eden—red-scarved and hollow-eyed—had worn after the party. The photo immortalizes the day Eden and I went apple-picking with their little foster siblings in the orchard by the dome's southeast curvature. The children's home shut down during Era-1 of the Virus. I suppose Kronos was too busy building prisons to bother with a new shelter for its children.

There were other, private photos too that I revisited with self-harming frequency during our separation. Eden posing naked for me, their jellyfish mod dancing wildly over their heart, flushed warm with blood.

The on-set bustle climbs its boisterous peak, then plateaus. I hurriedly flick my holo-screen closed while

Axiom lets her heavy, silver-thread robe pool at her heels for a crew member to collect. Then, she takes a seat across from Evi. The lights lower and mellow, a confidential illusion saturating the set. The perfect host, Axiom no longer acts fearful of Evi. She leans close across the flimsy table separating them. Even from my perch in the wings, I can see the hunger in Axiom's eyes—that of bottomless curiosity.

"Evangelia," Axiom says, all warm and reassuring. "The new cyber-sensation, the girl brave enough to step forward and share her tale. The scandal of the laboratories and correctional facilities—unveiled?"

My sister laughs. Relaxed, relatable, the perfect daughter of Kronos. "Evi is fine. And I don't know about brave, Axiom, but I do hope what I say today will pry open some willfully sealed eyes. Suffice to say, we weren't the only monsters inside the facilities."

My sister speaks, and like the performance at March's mansion the other night, she has the whole world rapt. Bewitched. This is no Eater magic. There is no Eater magic. It's all Evi's own charm. At school, she pretended to be vapid and unintimidating, leaping from partner to polycule and always minimizing herself. As if, by occupying as little space as possible, she would be rendered easier to love. Yet Evi's always been the smartest person I know, equal parts manipulative and earnest to a fault.

"Our affliction is not contagious, never has been," Evi says, focused on Axiom rather than the hive of camera bots hovering in her face. "Some of us simply changed the day of the Quickening—we acquired an organic need for a diet of meat. We cannot turn others, even if we wanted to. But still, the media were quick to call it the Eating Plague and turn the common opinion against us. It made it easier to lock us up without guilt amid the Era-1 chaos and confusion."

The live crowd boos or cheers from their holo-projections. I run the audience statistics, itching to deactivate the fake heckler accounts but wary of drawing attention to myself.

My sister talks about the black vans grabbing people from the streets as test subjects. The cat-and-mouse games that hazard-suited doctors and armed guards played with the inmates. Gnarly hypotheses of sterilized excisions tested and retested in the name of science. Even the Crimson Ribbons weren't safe from the White Coats, though Healers had not metamorphosed into monsters—merely into the ones keeping the monsters alive. It was a mutation nonetheless, and Kronos doesn't forgive aberrance in its children.

I remember the Quickening: gasoline and gore and gutters gathering flies, red remains like rotten flowers. Young people crouched behind overturned cars or trash cans—eating or healing or hiding from it all while they cried like newborns. And the smoke rose, and the dome lowered to seal us all inside Kronos' hungry belly, so no one could breathe without choking on red smog and meat and grief. Then, the unQuickened took things into their own hands, pouring into the streets with rifles and metal pipes. I hid behind four walls while the city bled from every wound. The city burned for days. And when the fires were put out, the bodies were collected by the cleaning bots, and the rogue Eaters were locked away, oubliette-deep.

The city washed its hands of our strange, new hunger.

"The place where they kept me was the most brutal of the bunch," Evi says, the fluttering movements of her hands like mourning doves in the studio's air. Her voice, too, is torn to shreds as tears stream down her cheeks "Our biology was studied, our bodies vivisected. Yet they seemed to forget, these scientists of Kratos, that the pain we felt was as real as their research."

I can't tell if Evi's tears are genuine or affectation. I thought I knew my sister better than anyone, but seven months apart is enough time to unlearn someone at the end of the world. And if her tears are real, then so was every incident described inside the facilities. All because of me.

An infrasound vibration alerts me to March's encrypted message through my holo-tab. With one last glance at Evi's tear-streaked, nacre-gleaming face, I leave the studio and throw myself into the backseat of another one of March's self-driving cars. The doors lock behind me as the car glides soundlessly down the bustling streets of Kronos. I hate that I can't leave once I enter these contraptions, hired and controlled by March. I could mess around with the car's code, just to see if I can override command—

No. If I am to change things up in Kronos, I need to let go of my natural mistrust. Show March good faith.

I stare out the window. One neon billboard boasts in ever-changing font: Child acting strange? Let us know; let us help. Under it, slithering graffiti scrawl: the unquiet Quicken first. I cannot tell if the phrase is meant as accusation, or reclamation. Shuddering, I look away.

There are no parties in March's mansion this early in the day, but some stragglers—smudged makeup and molted glitter—sprawl across the front-room couches among old party detritus. They nurse hangovers or nap together like puppies in a litter. It's a bit Victorian, this display of decadence. A rich girl's idea of a revolution.

But perhaps I'm not giving March enough credit. Hasn't she created a safe space for the Quickened to let loose, meet our like, rebuild and organize without judgment?

I meet Eden outside of March's office. They are dressed in a black lace frock and an inability to meet my gaze. I wonder which of the many guest rooms in this labyrinthine house belongs to Eden now. Before I can say anything to my former best friend, the door to March's study swings open. Not by any sort of long-distance automation, I realize with a blink of surprise. March opens the door herself, giving an odd little bow as she welcomes us inside the antiquated space.

I study March's immaculate suit and stiff posture, and struggle to picture her either as a child, or a captive. But I suppose even March couldn't evade Kratos's might. She, who inherited this mansion and all its trappings from parents too wealthy, yet too dead to save their only daughter from the correctional facilities. Evi hasn't been the same post-Kratos, either. She was a wild child before but took care of me when our parents wouldn't. Now, I often catch my sister cackling or crying or crooning to herself after a Psychopomp injection. With the drug's pre-programmed hallucinations pumping like restless spirits through her veins, she stares at sunrays and moonbeams, taps random codes on our apartment's walls. Fairy-bound, as our dead grandma would have said. March is doing better than my sister in the aftermath of the Quickening. After all, she has the means to finance several parties, and several revolutions.

"So," I urge, memorizing the lavish layout of March's office to avoid looking at Eden as they take a seat beside me. "Our mission."

"Your mission," March repeats, "is to infiltrate the correctional facility where Evi and I were held. You will enter Kratos as Crimson Ribbon contractors. Someone on the inside will help."

"No," I grit out, my nails digging into my wing chair's green leather arms. I want to reach out to Eden, but I don't know if my touch would be welcome on their tensed shoulders. I don't want to give March more ammunition than she needs. "Kratos is the worst of the facilities."

I doubt even the Crimson Ribbons—mediators keeping us from another city-wide upheaval—would be offered enough protection within Kratos' walls. The city does nothing to snuff out the public's disdain, the jeers, and the judgment toward its on-duty Healers.

"Oh, but haven't you heard this is the reformation era now?" March asks. Her laughter is as bitter and sharp as swallowing perfume. "After all that lab-rat torture porn got leaked? Kratos is peddling a brand-new image of hope and rehabilitation. No more starving the sick and needy! They bring Healers in now instead of only feeding us rotten meat from Gods-know-where."

She slams her fist on the heavyset oaken desk. It's the first emotional display I've witnessed from the ever-unwrinkled March. Her outburst makes her more real in my eyes, and it causes Eden to jump. They always were skittery. Shit parents and an endless rotation of foster homes sent my best friend seeking refuge in my bedroom at all hours. I knew how to protect Eden then: playing with their hair to the tune of immersive neo-synth-pop, entertaining them by hacking the neighborhood surveillance system, sucking them off until they wept.

But now, I don't know if we can protect even ourselves.

We have a mission, Eden and I: Reconnaissance, cyber breach, data collection. We must squeeze through dark, dangerous places like my copper-wire centipede. And we must pray to the city's gods that we slither out unseen if we want to live another year under the dome.

"Alright, Jonah," Eden says before I can speak. Their voice feathers and fissures, but they carry on. "The facility—I imagine you have the blueprints of the place?"

March nods, restored to her unruffled self at whiplash speed. "My inside informant has provided everything we need, including two Crimson Ribbon access passes. You will visit Kratos twice a week, as many times as it takes. While Eden caters for the inmates—" March turns to face me "—you, Nora, will enter the laboratory. Get your copper-wire plaything to reveal what Kronos and its scientists have kept hidden from the public."

I remember Evi's earlier speech. "You don't think it's a virus," I say, rolling the realization on my untasting tongue.

March shakes her head. "It manifested simultaneously under all twenty-six domes. The cluster-cities don't have that type of inter-communication network. It would be antithetical to their sustenance-and-preservation ethos." She's right. Travel between cities is prohibitively expensive and paperwork-heavy to avoid emissions, and so is trade—not that this ever stopped March's relatives from importing all these antiques. "Whatever the Quickening is, we must find and reveal it before Mayor Pappas gets re-elected. Otherwise it'll be too late for us."

In response to the spike of my heartbeat, my copper-wire centipede slithers out of my shirtsleeve where it's been nestling, charged by my body heat. March's keen eyes land on its slender, segmented body. I let my copper-wire centipede crawl across March's desk, darting in and out of her fountain pen cases that must have cost a fortune. Although my centipede's patent might fetch a good sum if I were to sell, my prototype cost next to nothing. It is made of mismatched, broken parts, just like I feel sometimes.

"Incredible," March says, her snake mod reaching out to meet my robotic centipede that will snatch all the sensitive biomedical information she is after. "Evi said no one but us four knows about your invention. But to think you never auctioned this to the highest bidder...."

I don't like how she stares at my centipede like something to own. Am I a tool to her like my copper-wire treasure is? What about Eden? Evi?

March holds the centipede in her open palm, watching between paternal and clinical as my creation wiggles against her fate line. I have this vision of March's fist closing, crushing my prototype.

But she only hands it back, the copper warmed by her touch.

"Soon, you'll be able to use this many-legged marvel of bio-engineering. I shall arrange for the lab to be empty and give you and Eden proper alibis. And you, Nora, will give me what this world needs most."

With a curt wave of her hand, March expands her wristband's holoscreen, signaling the end of the discussion. The talk show where I last left my sister projects itself between us. Evi looks poised and pretty, even with tears brimming her eyelids. She is a tragic, beautiful martyr figure.

"We just want to heal and rebuild what was broken in the Era-1 riots," Evi says, hands clasped like a penitent above her chest. "We want a chance to prove we can do better than the day of the Quickening."

I seek Eden's gaze for the first time since entering March's office. They meet my eyes unflinching, and for a stretched-sweet moment, we look on. I want to prove to Eden, too, that I am someone who no longer runs away from what I've done. Someone they can trust to have their back in Kratos, and beyond.

"Alright," I tell March, whose eyes never once depart from Evi's projection. "We will enter the facility. I will do what needs to be done."

STEPS FOLLOW ME down the rose-strewn garden path of March's mansion. My skin prickles before settling—the footfalls are as familiar as my own.

"The plan," Eden pants once they reach me. Their cheeks blush the same dusky color as the roses wreathed around the iron gate that opens onto the street. "Shouldn't we discuss it now we're working together?"

I study Eden. They look unsettled, not knowing where we stand. Perhaps a bit lonely, too. Reflexive of their proximity, something in me responds. A feeling that isn't eros, but philia, agape, and storge, all wrapped up in regret like the twisting, thorned stems we walk under.

I let Eden lead me down the road, then off onto a paved street of quaint trinket shops and cafés. This is one of the few affluent areas of Kronos where the sparse, stout buildings do not choke the skyline, and the paths unfurl airy and verdant. March's mansion falls away from the looming horizon as we enter the first coffee shop that catches our eye.

Eden and I both wince as we realize our mistake. One by one, we must stand under the door detector, having the ID chips of our wristbands scanned. I hold my breath as I cross, but the overhead mechanism doesn't beep, an indication that an Eater has entered the establishment. Evi's sacrifice protected me yet again from cruel or curious gazes.

At the automated self-service counter, I swipe my creds-chip for two coffees and a few sandwiches for Eden. They need the nutrition since they regularly donate meat. Even with their bodies' rapid regeneration, working Healers still need triple the usual calory intake to function. It can't be cheap, and the city won't reimburse the Crimson Ribbons for their labor—another one of the reasons Eden needed March's patronage. That, and March taking Eden in after Evi was locked up, and I secreted myself away with my shame.

I am reminded of the times before the Quickening when I found Eden camped out behind our school after running away from yet another foster home. How I told them: You're staying with us from now on. But I can't expect Eden to want to follow my direction anymore. We've grown too far apart for that. Doesn't matter that I want them near me, and not just because we are about to infiltrate Kronos' most infamous facility.

When I hand Eden their food, their eyes widen.

Shocked, then pleased. Our hands touch, their mouth opening to—

"Hey, meat-sack!" a boy in line hollers at Eden, snickering with his friends.

Eden's fingers fly to the red scarf around their neck. I clench my fists and grind my expanding teeth, incandescent on their behalf. But Eden shakes their head, wild eyes shifting. Scared that, if I do anything to defend them, I will reveal my unregistered status. And then I'll be in Kratos as an inmate, and March's plan will have failed before it has begun.

"Should I start wearing a ribbon when we're together?" I ask once Eden and I have claimed a remote table, far from the watchful crowd. "Safety in numbers and all that?"

"You don't have to. Not outside Kratos, at least. I just..." Flushing pink, they play with the Crimson Ribbon before untying it, neatly tucked into their purse. "It feels comforting against my skin, so sometimes I forget I'm wearing it."

Warmth suffuses me. I remember when Eden asked me to buy them a collar: a dainty, velvet little thing. They used to wear it around their throat and knew it was my gift. A promise of my devotion and extension of my touch. And now, where Eden once welcomed the careful-squeezing grip of my palm, they carry the scars from my canines, too deep even for their newly manifested powers to heal.

We sit in silence. Eden polishes off their food to regain their strength. I pretend to sip my tasteless coffee—a decoy in case anyone wonders why I'm not drinking; if I'm perhaps not normal, if I'm one of them.

The truth is, I was the city's unquiet youth even before the Quickening. And now, this new appetite gnaws on my belly; the laws hound my every step, even with my relative protection. My strange transformation was thrust upon me by environmental factors the laboratories' unscrupulous experiments have yet to determine. And with Eden here, I have more stakes than ever in March's revolution. Still, I cannot unclench my claws from my cowardice.

"I don't know why March unsettles me so, but she does," I confess, my skin prickling pyretic with my shame.

"I have a theory, but you won't like it." An impish smile plays upon Eden's lips. The first flicker of mirth I've seen in them post-Quickening.

I twirl my soggy paper straw. "Let's hear it."

"Well, you and your sister always had a weird psychosexual dynamic on account of growing up all alone and wild. So, Evi's first serious girlfriend makes the possessive part of you bristle."

"Shut up," I spit out, laughing despite myself.

They aren't wrong, exactly. My sister and I have cycled through god complex, codependence, and maladaptive daydreaming—presumably from growing up without adult supervision. While our parents gallivanted all over Kronos—the miracle city of their own parents' dreams—they left only an electronic nanny to look after us. I'd taught myself how to hack that old robotic model by the time I was nine, having it show our parents a pre-recorded feed of us quietly playing or studying. In the meantime, Evi and I pranced about performing pranks and petty crimes like two feral kids out of a fairytale. Evangelia and Eleonora, Evi and Nora. Always together.

Did Evi really keep Eden from me to punish me for Kratos, the price I paid for allowing her imprisonment? Or could my sister be envious of my former bond with Eden? Evi used to call me a prude for not seeking any sexual or romantic partners, at a time when our generation rejoiced in rejecting our parents' pleas for virtue. However, I always suspected Evi secretly enjoyed having all my attention to herself. Then Eden came along—not changing my sexuality, but charting with me its unseen fathoms. And, perhaps, make Evi feel replaced—enough for her to ensure all I did for months was hide and await her homecoming.

But it's not right: Evi hiding Eden; me distrusting March. It's not healthy.

"I know March and I both Quickened into Eaters. But sometimes she will look at me and—" An embarrassed giggle escapes me. "I'll feel like a field mouse facing her snake tattoo."

Eden nods. "I know what you mean. Jonah can be… intense. Ask her about it sometime. You're not the only one with a weird upbringing, you know."

"When March feeds…" I start, then trail off. "No, forget it."

When she feeds on you, is she careful? Does she hurt you? But what right do I have to ask this question? To want Eden out of March's lavish roof and under mine? I have yet to prove myself the safer choice. Perhaps even that reasoning is wrong; I am too close to how Kronos views its Healers as poor, broken victims and the Eaters as vicious, broken beasts. My months-long isolation didn't seem to shield me from absorbing all the new stereotypes about us.

Eden sighs. We both lapse into viscid silence. From a nearby table, two prepubescent girls watch a holo-video with the volume just loud enough for me to hear my sister's husky voice. I gesture at Eden to be quiet, and we both listen.

"That poor girl," one of the pre-teens says. "No way to contact her sister from inside the facility."

"It wasn't her fault the Virus took her," the other girl replies, hugging her friend close.

Those kids had been too young to be affected by the Quickening. And now—thanks to all the Quickened subjected to unethical experiments—they have a vaccine that prevents another spontaneous genetic mutation. Yet my sister's words still touched these kids. What if there are others like them? What if March's plan and Evi's media campaign are already working?

And I—what if I have it in me to be a part of it all?

The pre-teen girls finish their drinks and leave the café hand-in-hand. Eden and I stay seated, staring dazedly at each other, long after they are gone. We leave at closing time, each heading their separate way—but not before I make sure the closed-circuit ID-tracker over the café's door malfunctions.

PART II
PALIMPSEST /
PSYCHOPOMP

N THE SMALL hours, I pore over the Kratos blueprints, a migraine rattling my skull.

My affinity for computer science and robotics, combined with the free rein afforded to the parentless, made me skilled at forcing entry through interfaces and databases. It was a puzzle, a riddle that soothed my bristling brain. By high school, I'd perfected the prototype of my copper-wire centipede, and my hacktivism was helping my classmates get rid of bullies, retrieve leaked nudes, or erase embarrassing incidents from the web. I'd even accessed Eden's foster agency file, altering their criminal record of petty vandalism around Kronos.

So why did I not help my sister inside the correctional facility? Why didn't I join forces with an advocate group to fight for better conditions for the Quickened? I could have been an asset to the revolution long before March.

Instead, I spent seven months in self-exile. Missing Eden, the best friend I went from adoring to devouring. Evi, who I'd never had to live without. I even missed my parents, gone on a VR vacation to a sibling-city and unable to return during the Era-1 quarantine, then unwilling to face their monstrous daughters. The only visitors to my increasingly filthy apartment were my Crimson Ribbon regulars. The only comfort I allowed myself was the aftercare after a Synergy-booked feeding session.

Perhaps my inaction went beyond fear of discovery. After what I'd done to Eden, part of me thought we did not deserve to be saved. I know better now. Even scientists acknowledge that there was nothing those affected by the Virus could have done. We were like bodies controlled by parasitic fungi, animated by vestigial instinct, while our minds watched on, terrified, paralyzed. And still, the city thought only the bad kids— the wild kids—got struck by the Quickening. Those of us who deserved no mercy in the aftermath.

I refocus on the blueprints. The bare-boned holding cells and isolation rooms are too small for a person to lie down fully. I know Evi spent such a long time there. I pinch the holo-projection like a fold of fabric, then flick my fingers to zoom in to the feeding bays, where Eaters were strapped head to toe before a piece of stale meat was shoved between choking lips. I inspect camera routes and guard shifts, motion sensors, and inmate schedules.

Finally, I memorize the way to the medical lab, where the experiments had taken place. This is where I'm meant to eventually plant my copper-wire centipede while Eden acts as decoy. Any material I retrieve, March will use to extort the Kronos officials and influence the next mayoral elections. Keep us from losing the few rights we have managed to win back.

Though I still believe this is some rich girl's revolution, I can use the resources March provides me. Cause a tumult in Kronos' belly. Cause a change. My task is less visible than Evi's media campaign but so much more damaging if my cover is blown right into the belly of the beast.

My sister may refuse to speak to me about the facilities playacting at reformation, but I watched her talk show. I have seen the leaks. She dreams of Kratos still. Awakens shaking and screaming, then laughs and pretends nothing happened in the morning.

Earlier, in the blue-lipped night, I peeked into her bedroom. Evi's limbs jerked in somnolescent chase, blankets a sweat-damp heap on the floor. I used to do this when I was younger: stare into my parents' room as they slept, willing them not to disappear, watching for the rise and fall of my sister's chest to make sure she was still here. She was not leaving me alone.

I glance at the red-dyed ribbon on my desk next to the collection of monitors and hard drives. Then, I stroke the scarf between my fingers like a silken river of blood. Practice wearing the crimson ribbon in the mirror and disperse all thoughts of meat cuts wrapped up in pretty bows.

The Healers did not choose nature's hand any more than we did. I know the common taunts: pain-junkies, meat-sacks, monster-enablers. Yet the Crimson Ribbons are the only ones who give a damn about keeping us fed and free of the dreadful facilities. So, tomorrow, I will wear this ribbon with pride and will match Eden step by step into my sister's nightmares.

A LASER-ENGRAVED SIGN hangs over Kratos' gates: ἐλεύθερος γὰρ οὔτις ἐστὶ. No one is free. Yet the correctional facility, named after the winged enforcer of power in its rawest form, promises to deliver us from our hunger by starving the beast within.

"Do you need a Tran-Q pill?" Eden whispers as we stare into the cyclopean red eyes of Kratos' cameras, waiting for a gate guard to collect us.

The crimson ribbon wraps twice around my neck, tightening with my hyperventilation. Eden is a calm, steadfast flame by my side. They don't wear their usual sundress but jeans and a V-neck shirt, taking comfort in androgynous ambiguity. I'm sweating in my button-down, struggling to keep my expression neutral.

I shake my head. "I need to be alert." Despite the twin ribbons around our necks, only one of us is a real Healer. I need my wits intact to maintain our cover.

My eyes shift about. Across the street, a cluster of anti-Healer protestors wave placards depicting red-hued ribbons torn apart. They shout that we're going to hell for enabling the wickedness of the Eaters and sullying the temples of our bodies.

"Don't they know if the Healers let the Eaters go hungry, there would be no one left for the stupid dome to protect?" I hiss.

Grimacing, Eden faces away from the protestors while hunching with the weight of each stare. My anger is a chafing noose. Without the Crimson Ribbons, the fraught new peace of Kronos would collapse. The city officials have tried to spread the slogan Blessed are the Healers to coerce more Quickened into duty. Yet the sight of a Crimson Ribbon working for those in need is often met with slurs and sneers.

The front gates unlock through a plethora of buzzes and clicks. This is a multi-sealed mechanism I could never hope to crack on my own. A robotic attendant accompanies us through a drab corridor into the guard room. The bot has a chest pouch of sleeping gas in case we act suspicious enough to trigger its sensors. I force my breath to even out, send a prayer to Titans I only half-believe in and do not flinch when the smirking guards search us for weapons and contraband. High-voltage, AI-aim stun guns bulge from their uniforms' holsters. The centipede curled in the bio-engineered pocket under my tongue twitches in response, sanguine-tasting and undetected. On our way out, the guards snicker about the scars on Eden's neck. Something about damaged goods. I clench my fists but do not blow our cover.

Our stiff footsteps echo as we walk, chaperoned by guards. Kratos' triple-locked guts are lined with dull metal and gray-washed plaster, everything overlooked by state-of-the-art surveillance. Under the stark glare of too-white lights, there's no room for frivolities here. I vow to no longer judge March for her mansion full of textures and colors, luxury and indulgence.

Along the narrow row of cells, Eaters press against the reinforced glass, observing our procession with curiosity and longing. Some bang fists against the doors while others bite their lips to bleeding tatters. The facilities are reformed now after the first journalist allowed inside Kratos unleashed a scathing tell-all a month before my sister's release. To think this—the menacing guards and the hungry faces—is the improvement on the previous Era's conditions...

When Eden squeezes my hand, my cortisol-drunk brain grows even dizzier with relief. I know it means nothing. But the touch steadies me enough to focus on what needs to be done: keep returning here with Eden while we establish our cover, scope out the facility, and wait for March to create the right circumstances for the planting of the centipede. In the meantime, do not get caught.

Do not fall apart thinking: This is where your sister lived for seven months.

The pair of guards lead us to the feeding bay. When a commotion breaks out from somewhere deeper into Kratos' guts, one of the guards—hand to her gun—runs in the direction of the noise. Only one guard remains, bearded and uniformed, devoid of all mods per Kratos' regulations.

"We don't have much time," the guard gruffly addresses us. March's informant. He doesn't offer us a name, and we do not ask for one. "Go through the door. I don't care what you do in there or who does the feeding, but by the time you walk out, two Eaters must have fed."

Panic-winged, my gaze flits to Eden and finds them already staring. An Eater feasting on another is taboo among us: something unspoken but occasionally performed between the closest of lovers. My meat contains no nutrition; my body has better regeneration abilities than most, but I'm no match for the Healers. No, Eden must donate flesh for two.

We enter the feeding room, and the door locks behind us. There are no safety precautions for the hired Healers. The guns are to keep the Eaters in line and obliterate all thoughts of escape. Perhaps the mission would have gone smoother with a dose of Psychopomp—a VR illusion of happier memories superimposed over callous Kratos— pumping through my veins. But the least I can do is be present. Bear witness. Help however I can.

Two benches have been pushed against opposite walls inside the claustrophobic space. An Eater is seated on each bench and their ankles are secured to the metal legs. This is the so-called compassionate approach of the Era-2 facilities. No full-body binds and force-fed meat, but Quickened youth still treated like wild animals who could lash out any second. The Eaters are both male: one our age, with a dark fringe shielding vacant eyes; the other can't be older than sixteen. One of the youngest known cases.

The media painted twisted tales of a reckless generation corrupted by body mods and the blurred lines between sex and gender. Yet most of the Quickened were just regular kids. Kicked out and punished by their parents, locked up for something they couldn't have controlled.

Eden introduces themself and then asks for permission before sitting by the dark-haired Eater. There's no fear in their eyes as they offer a handshake and a smile. Eden is good at this job, I realize. Good at balancing reciprocal comfort. Despite his eyes' needful sheen and protruding teeth, the dark-haired youth doesn't go straight for a bite when Eden bares their shoulder. They chat for a bit, the young man's voice, unused to much talking, is creaky as old bones.

I sit on the other bench next to the younger teen.

"Hey," I say. "I'm Nora. My friend is going to help you, but I'm afraid you'll have to wait just a bit."

Restless in his seat, the boy nods and redistributes his scrawny weight. "I'm Ananias. Do you have any tattoos? I keep sketching my body in blue ink, but the orderlies make me erase the tattoos before bedtime."

I tap at my wrist, where my extracted jellyfish once rested while nuzzling at my veins. The kid's unkempt eyebrows arch in sympathy across his too-thin face. "I get it. You had to cover yours to stay safe."

He sounds older than Kronos, though his voice cracks high with growing pains. Some cognitive dissonance crystallizes inside me. All the young Eaters partying in lavish dwellings and urban areas alike are only acting carefree and wild to outrun the horrors of the past seven months.

Across the bench, the fringe-haired Eater shily edges toward Eden for their feeding. Eden tilts their body to shield the young Eater from view. I look away, embarrassed. Eden's mellow personality has been tempered in our time apart. This Eden exudes an aura of calm, asserts restraint, and doles out reassurance. I can see why the city fears the finesse and control that the Crimson Ribbons possess. The young Eater groans as he feeds, his hand coming up to cling to Eden's shoulders. Cuff marks girdle his wrists; the only modifications allowed inside Kratos are the violations to the Quickened body.

I turn my attention back to Ananias, clenching his teeth with longing as the meat scent coats our nostrils. My jaw locks at the memory of my first feeding.

I was sick. I was dying. I needed help. Help me quench my hunger, red, so red, oh please. Eden in my bed, daydreaming about us running away to a city in the sky where everything wasn't so tightly coiled and controlled. Eden shook me as I convulsed, my synapses crackling in polyrhythmic pain. What's wrong, Nora. What's wrong? My teeth reached for their neck like sickness and salvation both.

To distract us from recollections of past carnages, I draw Ananias into conversation until it's his turn to feed. He tells me he misses his favorite video games; without his old VR gear, he conjures alternate realities in his mind palace. Soon, he speculates which of his school friends turned into Eaters or Healers. We laugh, a sound the gray walls hungrily swallow.

Before I let Eden take my place on the bench, I ask Ananias, "Are there any messages you want me to deliver?"

Unlike Era-1, communication with the outside world is no longer prohibited. Yet guards often intercept correspondence and inspect it for risky ideas etched between the lines.

"Hey," the boy says so softly I can hear the cracks traversing my vitreous heart. "Can you tell my sister I'm sorry?"

BY THE TIME both feedings are over, Eden is swaying on their feet. Yet I sense their exhaustion interlocking with resolve, like snippets of code slotting into a sequence. A synergy of giving back to the Quickened.

I think about the data-collecting centipede I will soon be planting. How I, too, hold the power to slake my generation's famine for better days under the dome.

Eden taps on the locked door to summon March's guard. I wave goodbye to Ananias, who waves back. These are the Eaters deemed the most dangerous, incarcerated even after the facilities opened their doors for Era-2. Yet now I know these are just the kids no one's claimed, the ones whose families wouldn't forgive them in the aftermath. Nowhere to stay but within Kratos and its labs.

Eden presses down on a nanite gauze to staunch their wound, but the blood spreads faster than the flesh can heal.

March's inside man gawks at us. "Shit, you need to hurry before another guard comes along. They'll notice only one of you gave meat back there."

Eden looks at me, and their eyes distend with dread. How did we not think this through? We miscalculated; more proof that we are not performing espionage but playing spies. Young and small—insufficient.

Caught.

The guard exhales through his nose in Eden's direction. "Gods! Just slather some of your blood on her arm." When footsteps pound down the corridor, March's man shoves a supply closet door open and pushes us inside. "Do it quick!"

Our world swims tenebrous, aromatized by astringent cleaning solutions. The amorphous silhouettes of discontinued bots loom on the shelves all around us.

Eden pants with exertion, leaning sightlessly against a shelf. Some sundered metal part clatters, and we blaspheme under our breaths.

"Here," I say in the dark, steadying Eden by their unwounded forearms. "Lean your weight on me."

"It'll pass. Just need to eat my weight in calories and accelerate the healing."

Eden presses a hand against their nape's gaping wound, then smears their bloody handprint across my own neck. According to the blueprints, this tiny closet that has Eden and me infringing on each other's space is no bigger than the isolation room in which Evi was repeatedly thrown. This is the closest I've been to Eden since I embraced their newly Quickened body. Since I devoured.

"Do you hate me?" I whisper, their blood drying indelible across my skin.

"No." Eden's breath fans against me. "Maybe."

A half-sob wrenches from my throat. Evi always said I run cold, but my grief boils igneous enough to torch Kratos to the ground. "Do you wish I was the one locked up back there? You could report me; I wouldn't stop you if you wanted retribution—"

"No!" Eden erupts. A frothy fleck of spittle lands on my lips. I lick it away. "Can't you see I'm doing the opposite? The city wants us gone, so someone has to keep us alive. You're already a self-exile from your own kin. There's nothing I could do to you that you haven't already done to yourself."

It's my turn to pant now. To shudder with their words overtaking my system. The vehemence and the truth of it all.

A frenzied giggle tickles my throat when I ask, "So you don't want me imprisoned and tortured. Does this mean you forgive me?"

Eden laughs, too, delirious with endorphins and

blood loss. Then, sobering, they plant an impulsive kiss on my forehead. We stay crammed in the dark for a moment longer, each acting as the other's black mirror, sharing breath and blood and the unspoken burdens between us.

"No," Eden says eventually. "Not yet. I need to know you don't see me as a problem to solve and absolve yourself of guilt. And besides, you wouldn't stop wallowing even if I forgave you."

Their meaning ricochets across the tiny closet: You would not forgive yourself.

"Did anyone in Kratos hurt you?" is the first thing Evi asks once I've made it home.

Her glass-blown eyes are unmoored in some haze of dream or memory. Psychopomp. She stinks of rosewater from the injection, the Carrier of Souls taking my sister away from me to some manufactured moment in time prior to the things we've done and the ones done to us.

What do you care? the vindictive part of me rears up. You brought me into this. But I know there could be nobody else. I'm the only one who can pass as a Crimson Ribbon without my face being recognized from the facilities' database. The one with the wiggling centipede, ravenous for bytes of extortion material.

"No one bothered me," I say, while my too-tight skin screams, *are you certain?*

I think about Eden having to give away twice the flesh than usual to prolong our ruse. The guards, convinced we were Crimson Ribbons, treat us like dirt. Evi, who nobody will hire after the stigma of her confinement and with so few jobs reserved for humans rather than AIs. My part is such a small sacrifice. A speck compared to the daily tokens of humiliation Ananias and the rest of the Kratos kids pay. I will keep returning to Kratos until my copper-wire bug slithers through the necessary systems and gives voice to the synergy of the Quickened.

Yet the prospect of more visits brings bile to my esophagus. "Evi," I say. The word hangs beseeching in the empty apartment. "The facilities… Was everything you shared on air true?"

A desperate part of me hopes she was exaggerating to make the audience sympathetic to our cause and pave the way for March's revolution. The rest of me, who just walked through Kratos and back, knows she wasn't.

Unsteadily, Evi leaves the old sofa where she'd slumped after her Psychopomp injection and teeters toward me. I wonder what she's commanded the drug to show her when she stares at me. Perhaps how we looked when we were young and augmented and wild. My sister runs a finger down the decoy bandage on my neck and

Eden's dried blood underneath. Inspecting the flaking red particles, she licks her finger clean.

"You think I lied?"

You lied about Eden, I want to reply, but I have no right to antagonize Evi after she relinquished her freedom to preserve mine.

"It's just that you won't talk to me. I know nothing about what happened to you in Kratos."

Minute tremors span my muscles after everything I witnessed. And still, it must have been nothing compared to Evi's view of Kratos.

"Oh, Nora," Evi sighs. It's like she's not seeing me but my Psychopomp simulacrum. "I've been protecting you my whole life. Trust me—there are some things you'd rather not know. This is Era-2 of the apocalypse." My sister's thread-weaving fingers spider-crawl into fists. "Enjoy it while you still can."

I TRY TO sleep, but the city resounds with parties and protests, a pulse through a collective corpus.

Our world changed so rapidly eight months ago. The Era-1 riots might be over, but the city still thrums on the apotheosis of another upheaval. It shivers my bones.

Evi lies on the couch in deadweight slumber after restless hours of banging around the house—a ghost haunting the rooms she remembered from before her confinement. Once Psychopomp ran its course, my sister accused me of giving her clothes away in her absence. Everything was right there, unsold and unmoved, a shrine to her. But perhaps Kratos' scientists played with my sister's mind worse than I'd first assumed. When I tried to sleep, I woke up to my teeth tearing my pillow apart.

Silent so as not to wake Evi, I take the elevator down to the street level. I hail a self-driving car—our own car's parts having paid for the Synergy-booked feedings I needed to survive.

With every passing second, my skin ant-crawls; my limbs lurch with the illusion of being cuffed, injected, anatomized. Staying indoors is no longer an option.

Downtown, the city is awake and alert even as its officials try to sedate it into a complacent stupor. The city air crisps my airways: meat, trash, and artificially enhanced flowers. Lost in indecision, I pace along a strip of pavement, staring up at the curvature of the dome, nearly translucent in the nighttime. Until an ad appears—part of Mayor Pappas's pre-election campaign. The billboard of anti-Quickened promises swallows the better part of the dome. I shudder, thinking of all the Quickened too young to run against him, stripped of voting rights after their imprisonment. Nearby, on a sickly-looking tree, a sign boasts the motto Blessed

Are the Healers. Underneath, someone has jaggedly scrawled: Cursed the Eaters.

A mishappen bot the height of my kneecap bumps against me, beeping no loitering allowed. No loitering allowed.

I wander the music-blaring club district and late-night augmentation parlors lit in undulating neon, but nothing captures my interest. Everywhere is full of people making merry, yet I feel so lonely, so wrong in my shrunken skin.

Domed city Kronos. Miracle city Kronos. Devouring city Kronos. So, where does that leave me?

Eden was right. I cannot shake things up if all I ever do is punish myself for how I was made. Self-mutilated hands cannot rebuild the city's broken fragments. I need to learn to feel like more than a receptacle for my ravening. My guilt.

My feet have brought me to an after-hours yarn shop glowing lambent from within. Cannibal Support Group. The word on the hand-scrawled sign stops me cold. Nobody calls us that anymore; the word "cannibal" has been stripped completely from our collective lexicon. When I touch the door, it opens with a soft clink. No ID-detecting mechanism overhead—a safe space?

A group of young people sit on mismatched chairs around the tiny shop, surrounded by shelves of colorful yarn, spools of fabric, and baskets of long, slender needles. While I hover on the threshold, all eyes gravitate toward me.

"I'm so sorry, I'll leave...."

"Join us, if you'd like," says the circle-coordinator. Ey have the @ symbol gouged into the front of eir shaved head, wearing eir lack of gender as a proud, jagged scar. Too bad I cannot pare myself down and carve myself into the exact shape I crave. "My name's Polydor@. Anyone in this circle can choose to share or not."

I look at the rest of the Eaters in the group. Some are knitting or holding skeins in their lap for comfort. At the back of the shop, a young man curls on a beanbag with noise-canceling headphones and a drawing tablet. He waves at me but doesn't join the circle.

"Alright," I say. My body still vibrates with wrongness, no matter how I scrubbed at myself in the shower after Kratos. Perhaps this will settle me: seeing others of my kind free instead of fettered.

When I perch on a high stool, Polydor@ nods eir approval. I stay silent at first, trying not to fidget or feel like an intruder as the support group members share their tales.

A boy with blue roots and modified eyes stretching cyan tear-duct to tear-duct clutches the ball of yarn, signifying his turn to speak. "I was nearly eighteen, and my mom and I were fighting about university. I wanted to study marine biology by the sea domes, but she said it wasn't right to abandon my city. We were mid-argument when I Quickened. I chewed through her right cheek. The jawbone still gleams when she smiles now, saying how happy she is I stayed home to take care of her. How auspicious the timing of my monstering."

The one to take the yarn next is an Afro-Greek girl with box braids and opalescent piercings at hexagon intervals across her skin. "I was home when the Quickening broke out. Gnawing pit in my belly, red blare of the sirens—too many sensory triggers. I hid under my bed with the dust bunnies, pinched myself to wake from the nightmare. My partner found my hiding spot and fed me her flesh. She wasn't a Healer, but she still followed her instinct to keep me safe."

My throat constricts into a crawlspace the more stories are shared. There's no pity here. No judgment in the face of suppurating wounds.

"I killed my uncle," one of the younger kids says, curled-up knees hugged inside their chunky-knit sweater. "He was a bastard but all I had. A relief when the hunger came and let me do what I'd always fantasized. I walked into a police station covered in blood and viscera. Turned myself in. They took me to the facilities, treated me worse than he ever did."

Onward the circle goes while my ears whistle like a windstorm battering the dome. Then, it's my turn. I wring the yarn between my hands and stare off into the distance.

"I…" My voice is a croak. I swallow the thickness of my spit and try again. "I keep running away. I would like to learn how not to."

I think about Evi taking my place. Going to hell and back for me, her ungrateful little sister. Yet when I open my mouth, it's not Evi's name I expel.

"Eden. My—" best friend, queer-platonic partner, co-conspirator. "My Eden. I hurt them when I Quickened. And now they don't want my apology. Not unless I learn to live with myself first."

Polydor@ looks me in the eye with so much compassion it inundates my lungs. "We are not responsible for our Quickening," ey tell me. "But the people affected by us aren't responsible for forgiving us either."

I nod around a mouthful of tear-salt.

At the end of the share circle, there are no hand-holdings or affirmations, to my relief. While everyone mingles, a part of me wants to flee, always worried I am not worthy of love, or perhaps not capable of it despite knowing I'm aromantic, not heartless.

I stand before the yarn shop's bulletin board, studying the ads for Healer support groups; fundraisers for the Quickened wishing to flee to a different dome-city; trauma-informed Crimson Ribbons offering their services to Eater survivors of sexual assault.

It used to bother me that my peers seemed to have no cohesive, conjunctive approach to recuperating from the tragedy of the past year. Yet it never occurred to me before all the small, different ways my peers might offer or request kindness, in the form of paper ads—old-fashioned, untraceable.

Polydor@ walks up beside me, eir large frame a silent comfort stretching for several moments. Eventually, ey speak in a melodious tune. "Us vermin of Kronos take care of our own."

"You called it a cannibal support group," I say. "Why?"

"It's not a slur, just a descriptor. Sometimes, giving names to things is the best defense against Kronos."

I avert my eyes from the bulletin board, settling them on Polydor@ instead. Eir mod's interface makes the name's suffix blur with static in my head. A clever party hack.

"One of many gifts," I say, and Polydor@ laughs and nods.

"That's my name. So, what would you like tonight?"

I look at em, and wonder if I exude loneliness the way ey do confidence. "I don't know, what's on offer?"

"For you?" More laughter, mellifluous. "Two things.

Firstly, I offer the ocular lens to all the Quickened who come into my shop. Here."

Ey scan something into my holoscreen, an encrypted code which I transfer over to my implant's interface that hasn't been getting much use since the Quickening. I look around the yarn shop and a green calming ambiance surrounds the ocular lens and my vision. I look outside, and the swirling red-alert colors overlaying the street beyond make me cringe.

"The lens... it shows safety from danger," I realize, accessing the crowd-sourced information stream for each building. Each business. Each nook and cranny of Kronos. "Did you make it yourself?"

"Oh no, my Healer ex-girlfriend did while I was in Deimos." Deimos is the third largest correctional facility after Typhon and Echidna. "She wanted to make things safer for me when I returned. I am now paying it forward." A melancholy smile pulls at Polydor@'s pierced lips. As if remembering eir own superimposition of history. "She called the lens Palimpsest after the pages of medieval manuscripts written and erased while traces remained. Scraped again. Superimposed."

I turn Palimpsest off, then on again, dizzy with the enormity of the gift. "What about your second offer?"

Here, Polydor@ turns impish again, wiggling eir bulky shoulders. We head toward the beanbags and the young man with the drawing tablet and noise-canceling headphones from earlier. He introduces himself as Nikolas, Polydor@'s partner, shaking my hand while he leans against eir thigh. Like he doesn't need his headphones if his lover is there for him to press his ear against and drown out all sound but the lullaby of eir bloodstream. "We were about to head upstairs. There's an apartment there. Warm, quiet. You look like you could use some company."

I look at them both, considering Polydor@'s second offer. The thought of going back home to Evi is unpalatable. My skin does not hunger for contact, but there's something about the way Polydor@ and Nikolas look at each other—so tender, so effortless—that I want to bask in even from a distance.

"Alright," I say, and follow Nikolas and Polydor@ up the narrow staircase hidden in an alcove behind the shop's counter. The click-clack of the support group's knitting needles follows us all the way to the apartment. It's bohemian-retro and lit in a cozy orange ambiance; a pocket grown in the stomach lining of Kronos, hidden from the world.

Nikolas, a DJ at a downtown body suspension club, plays us a record from the analog collection his great-grandma brought to the dome-city in wooden crates. The singer's accented Greek slinks like a melodious veil between us. Nikolas dances by himself, but it feels like all three of us are dancing together.

Polydor@ smiles, soothing-green and lovely through Palimpsest's lens I've yet to turn off. "What are you comfortable with, Nora?"

"I just want to watch," I blurt out. I want to see the pleasure on their face, live through it vicariously. "No touching."

I wait to see if it's a dealbreaker, the not-touching. I've been asked before if I'm stone, and it's not that, not exactly. But Polydor@ does not press.

Eden and I have always been open within our relationship. Before, Eden would sometimes go out and fuck other people, then crawl into my arms afterward, smelling of the musk of their lovers. How sweet Eden sighed when they submitted to me cleaning and tending to them as they recounted their night out. Always, they chose to come back to me at the end of the day, still wearing the velvet purple collar I gave them.

Polydor@ smiles at me, shrugging off eir teal jumpsuit. Not a dealbreaker then. I nod back, slumping on a chair while ey take the pillow-strewn futon. When Nikolas gets naked, the low light burnishes his bionic leg prosthetic. He notices me staring and laughs. "Oh, relax, I lost my leg before you people went all cannibal on us. Got hit by a self-driving car years ago."

After my initial embarrassment, I laugh too. When Polydor@ offers me a rose-pink vial of unprogrammed Psychopomp, I take it. After Kronos' most recent sanctions, my generation has taken to programming the VR-drug to show us what mods and metamorphoses we can never attain IRL. My classmates used to love programming illusions of wings soaring over Kronos, the dome dissolving like a spray of cool mist over their pinion feathers, until the cluster cities—the prototypes, the Titans, the Olympians stretching from Athens to Thessaloniki—become nothing. Until our bodies dissolved too and only the beautiful feeling remained.

I add the coordinates, pre-arrange the illusion. In a perverse way, Psychopomp always makes me feel closer to my parents, who fucked off to their forever VR vacation. Left me and Evi behind. While Psychopomp works its rosewater-smelling, vein-tingling magic through my system, I lean back in the desk chair facing the futon where Polydor@ and Nikolas crawl on their knees toward each other. All glistening skin charged on friction.

I open my shirt and jeans and touch myself. I know I'm touching my genitals in real life, but through Psychopomp, I feel my nerve endings become blocked. Find only a blissful absence for my fingers to play with. My crotch is bare smoothness as I rub it. I circle where my nipples should be, but now, through the gift of unreality, only flat skin remains. My mind supernovas with pleasure all the same.

Yet I can't stop thinking about the sexless-mod dancers from Evi's homecoming. How their smoothness was permanent, while mine only an illusion. The mayor had brought a moral panic about the youths biohacking our sexual anatomies. Then laws passed to sanction body mods and implants. And when we monstered, people implied there was a connection between the mods and the Quickening. It was implied we biohacked our appetites to bring about the apocalypse that rent the city from within. Thus, was born the motto: the Unquiet Quicken first.

When Polydor@ smiles from the futon, the scar on eir forehead stretches, handsomely all-encompassing. I clear my thoughts to focus on the lovemaking scene before me, mentally gratified by the way the two bodies move. Mouths on members. Fingers in orifices. The spit and the slick of it all.

"Good boy," Polydor@ praises, sweat glistening on eir fat rolls, while ey ride Nikolas' blissed-out face.

The vulnerability of the act wheels my thoughts back to Eden. How they used to trust me with the breath in their lungs. The thought for once does not cause the surge of guilt, but a bittersweet nostalgia. To be the vessel of their pleasure, to see their reactions and know that I caused them.

The bodies on the futon shift positions. Nikolas comes up for air, gazing at me through heavy-lidded eyes. His hand goes to rub with purpose against the meat under his collarbone. "There's this thing we do," he tells me. "A recreation of the Quickening. But if you'd rather not be a part of it…"

I have heard before of people recreating traumatic events to reclaim them through catharsis. Pre-Quickening, Eden and I used to play all sorts of games. I will eat you up, I used to growl as they writhed underneath me, loving the smallness, the mammal-ness of it all. The calmness, afterward. But if we told anyone, we would be accused we invited the monstering upon ourselves by playing these predator and prey games.

For the longest time, it felt like we could do no right in the judging eyes of Kronos. The city that only knew to devour. And that was even before the Quickening upturned every rotten thing under the dome.

"Show me," I say, my voice going from breathy to breathless. The city invokes the smokescreen of bodily autonomy now when talking about protecting the Healers from us. But I can suddenly imagine no bigger show of power and agency than the willing giving of flesh.

Before my eyes, Polydor@ and Nikolas recreate the Quickening on their own terms. They take the meat-eating compulsion, the violent outburst, and tenderize it into eroticism. Polydor@ feeds on Nikolas gently, worrying his flesh between eir teeth like a kiss.

I watch closely their faces and bodies, but the thoughts exchanged through their feeding bond remain private. Still, I picture their exchange as I touch my featureless body. You taste so good. Thank you for feeding me. What can I do for you? I will burn Kronos to the ground before I let it hurt you.

I tighten my grip on myself, imagining Eden's soft curls and mirthful eyes. The blood, the games, the regret.

Then, Polydor@ fucks eirself on Nikolas with the blood pooling red and slippery between them. When ey kiss him, I know he must taste his own flesh on eir carmine-coated tongue. It only makes him ask for more. Nikolas clutches at Polydor@ like a dinghy in a storm. Like Eden and I once held each other.

When I come, it is small and without sound. Psychopomp dissolves like a rose loukoumi on my tongue.

"Let the camera bots see you," March hisses from the corner of her mouth. A smile is pasted on her face, so plastic it appears painful. "It's good to show your face here. Solid alibi."

I look around the harsh faces of those attending Mayor Pappas's pre-electoral rally. A city eating its children, and a mayor enabling the devouring. We aren't, after all, the only ones who hunger in Kronos.

This isn't exactly what I had in mind when March asked me to meet her out in the city for our debriefing, instead of in her study as usual. But, somehow, the scene about to unravel before our eyes is exactly what I expected from an anti-Quickened, anti-augmentation, anti-self-determination rally.

The clamor of bodies and bots becomes oppressive, even from the fringes where March and I stand. I turn on Palimpsest, Polydor@'s gift I've been using more and more since ey showed me how to read its database last week. Everything is red as danger here around the plaza, as the mayor climbs imperially onto the stage, preparing his re-election talking points. An old-fashioned electric mic awaits him—no voice-enhancement algorithm here like there was in Evi's homecoming.

March and I stand near the crowd, our faces seen but our words muffled as my soundproof field surrounds us. An illusion of safety soon to be broken by Pappas's speech.

Although we stand together, March still maintains a length of distance between us. I'd told myself I would make an effort to get to know March—for the sake of the revolution, but also my sister.

"You and Evi," I say, unused to making conversation after months of self-exile. "She said you two met in Kratos. So…"

"What was it like?" March asks though I'm not sure that's what I meant to ask. Perhaps something more childish, like, Were you star-crossed lovers? Did they keep you apart? Do you love her?

"Every moment of the day was accounted for. Fraternization was forbidden. Punishments swift and endless. A constant enumeration of our sins." She turns toward me. March's eyes are intense against mine, like two dark shards torn off the night sky. I sway, feeling as if I'm falling into them with every one of her words. Then, her bark of laughter startles me out of it. "So, just like my entire childhood, basically."

I stare into her canny eyes behind their wire-framed glasses despite myopia being easily treated. I realize March doesn't look at odds with the other rally attendees, with her old-fashioned clothes and behavior. Other than her underground schemes, the only rebellion about her is the snake tattoo darting under her starched-white, silver-cuff-linked sleeve.

This is the most personal detail March has shared with me about her life. I don't want to spook her, but I need to know. "You grew up religious?"

Not many people are these days, besides the superstition of honoring the gods and titans of antiquity after whom the domes were named. Keeping altars for them so the dome doesn't fall on all our heathen heads. But what March describes are the old-world, guilt-inducing ways of Christianity, the cults that segregate themselves from the newer, more progressive Orthodox parishes.

March chuckles, eyes trained forward to the erected stage. That perennially composed façade of hers sometimes makes me picture a lake of still ice: a mirrored shine on the surface with tenebrous fathoms underneath. I wonder what Evi sees when she looks at March. Someone who protected her in the correctional facility? Who ensured her freedom, financial security, and introduction to Kronos' news channels?

"Fundamentalists. My parents, rest their sorry souls, were part of a traditionalist sect—old money, old values. I went to a no-tech school, had a life path laid out for me from birth. Mom and Dad even gave me a boy name, hoping I'd embody the spirit of the son they'd always wanted."

"I'm sorry for your loss," I say, although her family and their church sound like abusive assholes. I sometimes forget that March is only twenty-six. An orphan like Eden, like Evi. Like me.

March waves her hand, tone acerbic. "I killed them both, of course, during the Quickening."

"Forgive me, I shouldn't have asked." I try to keep my voice down. My anti-surveillance software distorts our voices to the passing bots, but one of Pappas's voters might still hear. Then again, no one is looking our way, the crowd buzzing with its own indoctrination.

"It's for the best, really. They would have hated seeing me like this. Might have blamed my Quickening on demonic punishment for my daring to sully my body with my tattoo and my... predilections."

March's background explains the repression and old-fashionedness. The stiff, prim mannerisms cover many-faceted hunger underneath. For all her lavish parties, March never indulges. Always swathed in the shadows of her study and the weight of her parents' wealth and expectations. And another thing: I never see Evi and March together. Through good behavior or bribes, March got out of Kratos earlier than Evi. They've only known each other four months, maybe less. Perhaps they imprinted on each other amid all the hardships. Finding it hard to navigate their relationship among all the trauma and plans for revolution. Gods know Eden and I do not have a traditional relationship.

"There weren't many of us before in that church." March's sharp chin jerks toward the stage, where Mayor Pappas walks, crossing himself three times. "Of course, he's been doing his best to normalize traditionalism, and his followers eat it up."

I shift my focus back to the stage, while the rally attendees push closer to their leader. The silence feels weighted, pulsating.

"Aren't you tired of being afraid?" comes Pappas's

grandfatherly voice. It matches his brown tweed jacket. His bushy eyebrows and hair streaked in white.

My skin prickles on instinct.

His voters chant and clap.

Pappas speaks through the redness of my neural lenses, and something inside me—fermenting, festering—awakens at his words.

I remember when Mayor Pappas first got elected. Suddenly, custom-made gender transition became all that harder to access. Eden already knew they were transfem, but wanted no part in the binary, all-or-nothing transition Kronos offered them. For me, my lack of gender was so close to my lack of attraction as to become nearly synonymous, impossible to tell apart. Manifesting in my illicit desire for smooth, sexless skin. Together, Eden and I had watched from our holo-tabs as Pappas, at the height of his body panic campaign, said, "The trans people of the past were peaceful; they just wanted to match their bodies to their minds through transitioning. But these kids have no real dysphoria. They want to exchange their body parts for animal traits, tentacles, and cloacae, the new fad in my son's class. We cannot allow them to go running around like mutants, infecting the rest of our children."

I look down, and my nails have dug red indents into my sweat-slick palms. My ears are pounding. The mayor's words drift in and out of focus like a dizzy undertow. Until:

"It's clear the Quickened are a threat to the order of our city. So I ask you, what's stopping us from putting all those who mutated under their own dome and letting them, cannibals and meat sacks, battle it out?"

I feel like I've missed something, a stepping stone crumbled from under me, only to hit me in the face.

The crowd cheers. The crowd boos. Pappas continues, unstoppable. "Our ancestors figured out how to solve the food scarcity problem when they built these domes. So let the Quickened figure out their food situation by themselves so they can't corrupt the children of Kronos."

A voice shouts from the crowd—a Quickened journalist I recognize from my TabMe account. "That's not what we meant when we said we wanted to self-govern."

"Right! We never asked to have a battle royale under a new dome." A different Healer activist is saying this, but their voice, like their body, gets swallowed by the starveling crowd. Suppressed.

"The Quickened are our children," another person yells. They look in their forties, too old to have Quickened. An ally.

"Or what's left of them," calmly counters Pappas.

My heart staccatos. Stutters. Nearly stops.

There's a rumor about Pappas's own son Quickening. Being sent away to a sibling-city to hide his father's shame and hypocrisy from the world. A part of me wants to find that son, expose his monstering—but the thought of dooming one of my kin nauseates me.

"Era-1 was cobbled together far too hastily; Era-2 made too many concessions to monsters and their apologists. Era-3 must be swift and efficient in squashing the infestation of the Unquiet. This is what I promise you in exchange for your vote."

He goes on to describe biweekly meat-giving mandates for all Healers. Harder documentation and curfews for the Eaters until the creation of his unholy dome. His Tartarus, a death sentence for the so-called Eater and Healer renegades.

"I think we've heard enough, don't you?" March says eventually. Is she shaking, or am I?

I don't know what possesses me, but I attempt to comfort her with a touch on the shoulder. She flinches away. Just for a second, her eyes are that of a wild animal before she regains her composure. Is March like me, then, not wanting to be touched, ace or aro or both?

A new understanding dawns inside me, of why I never see March and Evi together as a traditional couple. It makes me less bitter to always be the one who picks up the pieces of Evi's increasingly erratic moods.

We turn to leave the rally, the last of the boisterous applause glancing off our backs. March is closed-off again after her earlier confessions. Her mouth tightens as she says, "In case you ever had any doubts about the plan. Now you know exactly what's at stake here."

I WAKE UP tearing my pillow to feathered, frayed bits.

I wake up biting my bottom lip bloody and ferrous.

I wake up and stare at the darkened ceiling, listening to my sister's night terrors like papercuts slicing over my eardrums.

I don't always think I can, but day after day—

I wake up.

THIS IS MY third time visiting Kratos, and I've had no luck releasing my centipede into the lab. By now, I know to save a bloody gauze from my Synergy feeding the night before and plaster it on my neck as a decoy. I carry water and snacks for Eden's emergency regeneration, something the correctional facilities are not keen to provide for the Crimson Ribbons, unlike the guards' regular abuse. While Eden donates meat, I sit with the cuffed Eaters—and talk.

Today, we exit Kratos to a chorus of chants. My centipede wiggles its wiry legs in response. It's not the anti-Ribbon protestors, but music mixed with recitations, rage comingling with revelry.

"Look," I say, pointing toward the two processions pouring through the streets. They arrest traffic and swallow the city's chrome-and-flagstone shop district.

The two protests—one of Eaters, the other of Healers—meet in the middle of the intersection. Then, like an ouroboros eating its tail, the two parades unite until they form a single deluge headed our way.

Some of the Quickened youths—masked and unmodded to evade drone detection—carry placards with Evi's moving face saying, "We want to heal." Others march under the banner of Synergy, the Crimson Ribbon app, chanting, "I choose who my flesh feeds." A response to Mayor Pappas's campaign to force all Healers into Crimson Ribbon duty. All Quickened under a single dome.

Eden stops one of the protesters, a Healer dressed all in red. "Is this about the pre-electoral rally?"

The Healer glances between Eden and me. "Like Pappas's people weren't degrading us enough day to day. Now, he wants us to be human cattle. No mention of salary or rights. Just meat!"

I gulp; Eden, in their red scarf and nanite bandages, shudders beside me.

An Eater swoops in amid the chaos to join our

half-shouted conversation. "There's talk of a secret Era-3 project to try and reverse the Quickening. People kidnapped from the streets into unmarked labs, now the media are monitoring Kratos and the like."

The Eater disappears back into the crowd's maw, which opens and closes, safely subsuming them.

Another Healer synchronizes his footsteps to us. He's in a sleeveless denim vest covered in peeling patches, unzipped to reveal the rainbow chest binder underneath. "Did you know those fuckers up on Kronos' top wanted to name us Givers? Healing is something you do for your body. Giving is something you do for others—you see where my anger comes from?"

His name is Orion, he tells us, barely twenty years under the dome and already disenchanted. "Then," he continues, "there are the religious nuts. Blessed are the Healers. Fuck off, maybe I want to use my power for myself!" He looks at me sideways. "No offense, baby."

I laugh; his vivacity is contagious. "What are you doing with your regeneration, then?"

In retrospect, the Healers obviously use their mutation for their own benefit. They are supplementary to us, yes. But becoming a meat donor is a vocation that should be freely chosen. Giving something up to gain something equal, like the no-genital performers from Evi's homecoming feast.

Orion puffs out his cheeks in contemplation. "Parkour. S&M down at the club. Car racing. I dunno, fucking… healing my bruises when my ADHD makes me bump into shit."

Eden exchanges holo-handles with Orion, chatting about a cyber-artist who razors art commissions into her skin, only to heal back into a blank canvas post-stream. I hope they meet up again. Eden should have friends who aren't Eaters. And friends who aren't me. Lovers, too, if they wish to. Then I remember we are no longer together, and I deflate like a punctured lung.

The protest veers into a corner, and Orion runs after it, yelling, "See you around, and don't let the White Coats get you!"

Without speaking, Eden and I hold hands and join the jostling sea of people. Like in March's parties, the air is charged with that wild, fearful euphoria. At any point, we could be carted away, back to the facilities or worse, if the mayor has his way. Chants resound from all directions, reclaiming the motto with which the city tried to stigmatize us. The unquiet Quicken first.

More than ever, I can see why the Quickened Eaters and Healers are in synergy with one another, not just symbiosis. Soon, even the unQuickened join us. The youth tired of being fearmongered into docility to avoid a bad-kid monstering. Adults whose charges were affected. Those who saw neighbor turning on neighbor, and who remember being young and confused, maligned and scapegoated. The whole parade stretches green and verdant through my Palimpsest lens.

Police drones zoom runic patterns overhead. Snapshotting every protestor's face to harm their job and housing opportunities or to post online in vigilante databases. As the crowd surges forward, I flick open my holo-screen and erratically type. The drones' red eyes turn black. Switched off.

And then, a third wave comes surging from the opposite direction. Steel canine leviathans arrive armed with rubber bullets and tear gas. Anti-Quickening protestors hide behind the police bots and their electrical shields, hurling their slurs at us unencumbered. The breath curdles in my lungs when I notice the young people among them shouting, "We will not be eaten."

Eden sways beside me with blood loss and the overheating press of bodies. After a quick blink of Palimpsest for the nearest safe space, I guide us inside a café, begging the tentacle-tongued owner for some sugar water to replenish Eden's strength. I'm still shaking with the rush of disabling those drones. Of marching hidden in the crowd, not because I was concealing my identity, but because I was part of a bigger, breathing whole.

Only when we've slid into a booth do I notice my best friend's shirt hem is wet with blood. "Eden, are you hurt?"

They don't stop me when I lift their shirt and trace my thumb over the bruised flesh around the gouge into their side. Whoever put it there, I can feel their hunger.

"It's not healing," I say, suppressing the urgency of my voice. "Was it from today?"

"Jonah needed to feed before I left the house." Eden hesitates like there's more to the story. "When she eats, it's like she forgets herself. She isn't violent but unfocused like she pretends she's anywhere else, doing anything but this. Her thoughts are all classical music— white noise through the feeding bond. She can't look me in the eye afterward. Or she weeps. Then, she's normal and unflappable again in seconds."

Eden lowers their voice. "I don't think March likes herself very much."

I compare this new information to everything I know about March, especially her religious childhood and my suspicion that she might be like me in her attraction and aversion.

"Leave March's mansion and come live with me. We can work on her revolution from my bedroom."

"The same bedroom where you killed me?" Eden asks, not without some humor. "But really... you're buying into the narrative that Crimson Ribbons are below you. It's a dirty job, they all think. Never mind that it keeps the city alive. With our history, you of all people should know I feel useful afterward, not used."

"I'm not asking you to stop," I say, taking their hands in mine. "I just need you closer, like we once were."

They always stayed with me before. When I said I loved them so much, I would claw my chest open and let them nest inside my ribcage, but I could not fall for them. I could have sex and savor every second of their ecstasy, knowing I had caused it—could lick away their tears of overstimulation and memorize their subsequent relief—but for me and my body, it would always be a distant, clinical act.

I have an unhealthy, codependent relationship with my older sister. I hack shit. I mistrust people. And still, I want Eden to choose me in the aftermath.

Screams ring out outside the coffee shop. I follow the drones on my screen, but the tear gas has already spread. Dry-eyed, we watch the procession of protesters and police. Once it's safe to walk through the rubble-covered, acrid streets, Eden comes home with me. And most nights after that.

I FLICK ON the living room projector for my sister's second interview. After Evi's talk show, forums erupted with threats and praises. Love or hate her, my sister brought the highest views to Kronos' smallest station, so others are clamoring to dissect her on air. Evi cannot afford to turn any invites down with Pappas spewing intolerance on every news channel.

While I wait, I auto-scroll my feed, every new horror settling stony in my stomach.

"Stop punishing yourself," Eden says, coming in from the kitchen with a plateful of protein. Due to all the feedings, they've been sleeping and eating a lot.

"Punishing? How?" I ask, not daring to look away from my tab in case I miss a snippet.

Rogue Eater gang named Arisen Gods calls the Healers the inferior mutation—scroll. Hestia's cult committing mass suicide to transcend to Elysium, far from energy depletions and civil unrest—scroll. Synergy's headquarters vandalized with algorithmic projections of slaughterhouse meats—scroll. The un/Quickened coalition labeled a terrorist organization after requesting amnesty for the initial stage of the Quickening—scroll.

Fear and suspicion disseminate through the news feed. I can feel them pulsate across the airwaves, fogging up Kronos' glass dome.

"You think this is your penance," Eden says, "for spending months uninvolved in Quickened issues."

It's not the first time I've done this, either. I used to watch porn to force myself to experience some flicker of attraction. I thought if I learned everything there was to know about sex, it would unlock the missing drive in me. My research made me stumble down all sorts of upsetting dark-web rabbit holes, from celebrity-lookalike sexbots to deepfake revenge porn.

Sighing, I switch channels, only to be met with an ad for 'your forever VR vacation', like the package my parents bought to escape their wayward daughters. Eden and I glance at each other, manic-giggling with the irony. Our hands rest between us on the couch. The jellyfish I re-installed under my skin after meeting Ananias at Kratos matches Eden's implant. Our jellyfish dance a languid pas-de-deux while waiting for Evi to appear onscreen.

Evi is dressed in a blazer and pencil skirt like something from our mother's closet. This time, the host is a man. When he arranges his too-perfect features—the only socially acceptable augmentation in a city obsessed with naturality—into a smile, it does not reach his eyes. My jellyfish undulates its tentacles in agitation as a pit yawns open in my stomach.

"Last time," he tells Evi in a debate-me voice, "you said there was a difference in your… appetites between the beginning of the Quickening and now. I find that hard to believe."

Evi's smile, held in place by several Tran-Q doses, wavers. "It was the first feeding. We were starving newborns.

Our bodies had just finished changing; they needed fuel, or they'd eat their own cells. There was no controlling it back then—Gods, none of us knew what it even was."

Eden and I shift on the sofa, uneasy. We remember.

Some chewed their own flesh to keep from hurting their household members. They were still sent away. Only those with families rich enough to protect them evaded the facilities or the crafty few who found another way out. But it's easy to blame the Quickened for every scarcity or structural issue in the city, the same way body mods and sexual exploration were once blamed for low fertility rates and a divergence from traditional family dynamics.

"And now?" the host scoffs. His hair is so sleek it looks brittle. "The meat still calls out to you, doesn't it? How are you people different than a rapist who cannot control their biological urges?"

The chasm in my stomach swallows me. Eden releases a pained groan beside me.

The camera bots capture close-ups of Evi's frozen expression. Evi is not unfamiliar with the plethora of date-rape drugs that circulated in our high school. I'd found her giddy and amnesiac after an outing, more than once, lamenting the holes torn into her favorite dress.

"What?" my sister asks the perfect-faced man across from her.

"You said you couldn't resist the hunger. So how are you... Eaters unlike a degenerate violating some unsuspecting victim in the street?"

Never mind that most rapes don't happen in random streets between strangers. Statistics of domestic and marital abuse will do no good here. This is an agenda to humiliate my sister, who's been gaining too much traction lately. A war with no bombs or battles to keep score. A bid to influence public opinion and the election's results.

"It's not the same," my sister stammers. "Humans aren't animals unable to harness their base instincts. They have logic, community."

The host smirks as if Evi walked straight into his logic trap. "You're saying you Quickened kids are animals, then?"

A scream strangles my throat as I flail for my holo-tab. My vision inflames a candescent carmine. Eden might be calling my name, but I'm too razor-focused tracking down this man, this smug scum's digital footprint. Predictably, his Cloud is full of incriminating photos of minors. Unpredictably, a link to his Cloud is shared with all his colleagues and viewers from a burner account. The screen blackens as the talk show cuts the signal to control the damage I just caused.

Eden holds me while I shake long after I've flicked off my holo-screen. They do not seem afraid of my rage, my hunger.

Eventually, the front door slams open. Evi is drunk, disheveled, mascara smudges spidering her eyes. I fuss over her, but she shrugs me off, glowering between me and Eden. She storms off to her room alone. Where is March after tonight's debacle? Does she not care to comfort her girlfriend?

Eden stares down at their scuffed combat boots. A defeated slope defines their shoulders. "I, uh, will leave you two alone. Might catch some of my regular Eaters for a session. Contribute to the household."

"You don't have to." I want this to be your home. But we both saw how that turned out last time when I repaid their trust by nearly killing them.

Eden grabs their red scarf with finality. I look at the front door closing behind them, then Evi's bedroom. For a tight-roping moment, I feel torn and bereft down to the eddying pit of my stomach and more alone than I've been since Evi came back from Kratos.

In the aftermath of the Quickening, many of us had to parent ourselves and each other to build cohesion where there was only confusion. The Crimson Ribbons were the backbone of this strange new world, with its strange new hunger. What keeps Kronos together isn't the dome, or the facilities' threat of power and control but the synergy of its people.

Yet, for the longest time, Evi and I only had each other.

"Evi?" I ask, hovering by her half-open door. "Are you alright?"

"No! I'm just so angry. All the gods-damned time. I never was like this before, Nora!" She lies in a scrapheap under the bedcovers, scream muffled into her pillow.

Once upon a time, my sister would laugh everything off: her exes' mistreatment, our parents' absence, her abandoned dreams of journalism. Evi would cry in between giggles, manipulate me out of emotional talks, and refuse to acknowledge our reality. She would balance on the edge of our skyscraper balcony under the starlit dome, and I always feared she'd ask me to override the anti-suicide nets because her smile glinted like it craved the freefall. Later, she would use Psychopomp to numb the pain through syringe-sized fantasies perfumed with rosewater and artificiality.

Evi never got angry. Until now.

"Jonah was the only one who saw my anger in Kratos. And she decided to do something about it. But now my own girlfriend is too caught up in her plans to even touch me. Am I really that unlovable?"

My sister sounds as broken as the world our ancestors bequeathed to us—this ruined land encased in unbreakable glass bearing the old gods' names. We get our crops and meat from Gaia, our fish and salt from Okeanos, but we are not post-food scarcity like the cluster cities want us to believe. Our domes' panels gather solar energy, but Kronos' overpopulated underbelly still lives in poverty.

They put a dome on us, called us fixed, and then wondered why we were so angry. Unquiet. Quickened.

Evi's slurred confession explains what she saw in March, how the two came to be. I have my theories about March—how maybe she's like me in the romance and sex realm—but my gut says Evi wouldn't appreciate my feedback. It's not exactly anger I detect in March whenever we meet—or rather, not only that. So many emotions twirl under her immaculate façade, like sluggish tentacles inside a lake iced over.

I slip into bed beside Evi, my heart molded against her spine. A simulacrum of when she would sneak home after school parties to cuddle and cry, You're the only one I trust, Nora; look at this hickey and that broken high heel and my broken heart. Later, when Eden shared a bed with me, Evi pointedly avoided my comfort.

"I dealt with that bigoted TV host." It's easier for us to talk like this. Harder to hide.

Evi sighs as my arms slither around her. "My sister. My perfect little savior."

"You keep hurting me," I blurt. Evi always brought out the petulant child in me.

"No. I'm building a world where you won't have

to hide in shadows and cyberspace. Our parents aren't coming back to their poor little flesh-eating daughters. All you have is me now."

"And Eden. I've always had Eden. Why did you keep them from me?" It feels good to finally ask, rip open the suppurating wound, and pray for the cauterization.

Evi only scoffs. There were times before when she doubted my relationship with Eden. Called Eden my plaything, not copper-wire like my centipede, but flesh-and-blood. Said: I have all this love in me that nobody wants. How can someone loveless like you bask in so much devotion?

"You don't know what Kratos was like during Era-1. For that, I am thankful. But don't I deserve to have you all to myself now after everything I did for you? My own flesh, my own blood. I needed you here with me, not running off with your little friend."

She's crying into her pillow again, but I don't have it in me to comfort her.

This is my sister who paces nocturnal trenches into the carpet, fights with her shadow, over-injects Psychopomp. By morning light, she will be talking about parties and revolutions. But this is the first time she's opened up about the facilities outside of a holo-projection. Hinted at horrors I've only ever encountered in password-protected sites. How inmates had to fuck the guards to be allowed some fresh air. How the meat was wriggling with worms, and it was either that or starvation.

This is my sister who lied to me. Despite knowing we would meet again at March's mansion, she kept Eden from me. She delayed the inevitable just to have someone with her after the isolation in the correctional facility.

"You let me think I was a murderer."

"Aren't you?" Evi asks, so gentle it hurts.

I try to leave, but my sister's hand snakes around mine. It holds me fast. At that moment, Evi is a little kid breaking her toys to draw everyone's attention to herself, and she needs someone to watch her so she doesn't tear herself apart.

I stay with her until she falls asleep, her tear-clogged nose snuffling through nightmares I'm too raw to chase away. Then, I go outside into the misshapen garden and wait for Eden to come home.

THINGS HAPPEN CENTIPEDE-FAST after that.

I take to sleeping during the day and staying up all night, fiddling with my centipede's code. I stand guard against Evi's nightmares. Wait up for Eden during their Synergy night shifts. Evi's social media blows up, as do her volatile emotions. Adoring fans show up at our door, while haters deliver feces through our drone drop-off zone. Once, a pig's heart still bleeding. I install more security around the apartment. My sister has become the face of the revolution. A pharma-trial-torture martyr sacrificing herself for a safer future generation. No more children monstering, the articles about her say. No more children eaten in the city of Kronos.

After Synergy bans Evi because of her overfeeding, I search for therapists who won't try conversion therapy techniques on my sister like Kratos' personnel did. March beats me, finding Evi an unregistered Healer. After that, Evi spends more and more time in the mansion, floating through the fantasy fingers of Psychopomp. She's only sober for her live appearances, even as she falls apart when the cameras are off.

When staying inside digs teeth and thorns into my skin, I wander the city, my feet cartographing Kronos. Through Polydor@'s Palimpsest, I watch my city burn red for every hateful establishment. Yellow for those too cowardly to pay the removal fines for the detection alarms. Green for small oases open to all. So many of their storefronts have been shattered and vandalized. Palimpsest exposes every rotten cavity under Kronos' tenuous peace and the front of forced civility.

Era-1 is over, but nothing has changed. The riots were suppressed, but the flames still roar in rage and choke every living thing under the dome.

The closer to the elections, the more the city thrums with unease, unrest. Every day, there are stories of attacks against Eaters and Healers. And on the conservative channels, deepfakes emerge of Quickened teens assaulting people on the street, feasting on their red-beating organs. I try to debunk as many as I can. But occasionally, one turns out to be real, a kid snapping under pressure, and debunking the artificial reels becomes a losing game.

Eden comes back from jobs the worse for wear. Blood and pus spread through their nanite bandages, the bags under their eyes bruise, and no matter how I stock up the fridge, they take longer to regenerate each time. We do not discuss the possibility of me feeding from Eden, even when Synergy prices skyrocket, while the profiles of the Andreadi twins and my other regulars vanish. I wonder if they left our cursed city or are just laying low to avoid becoming another statistic.

Our relationship is not back to what I broke, but perhaps it is evolving into something bright and brand-new. The more Eden and I orbit each other, the clingier Evi gets. I wear myself thin attending parties and protests, wildly oscillating between euphoria and despair, unity and isolation. I don't want to leave the city like our friends have. Yet...

"Perhaps we could... Get a ticket. Go somewhere,"

I reluctantly suggest to Eden. Polydor@ from Cannibal Support knows how to move fugitives between cities. I could help forge our papers. Ask Polydor@ to give Eden and me one final, selfish gift.

Eden shakes their head. "We just reclaimed Kronos and each other here in the end times."

I think about my parents, always running away. Coward daughter of coward progenitors. I hold Eden close in bed and pray to gods and titans to keep my best friend safe, or else.

A week before the elections, Eden comes home with broken ribs and a swollen-shut eye. One of the night cafés they frequent—deemed safe through Palimpsest's curated database—had been hijacked by a fringe group of unQuickened, who saw the red scarf Eden wore and thought, You heal, right? So, we can hurt you all we want.

Whenever I see March now, she is burning with a single-minded focus. A hunger for more than just flesh, like a candle eating itself with no regard for its own wax and wick.

We are all standing on the precipice. And we are teetering closer to the fall.

AND THEN, THE day comes when March approves the release of my centipede into the lab. I auto-schedule an email for Polydor@ with all my hacking cheat codes and robotics notes in case things go awry inside Kratos—in case I don't come back. Eden and I tie each other's red scarves for luck. Evi watches from the door, Psychopomp-detached, not making a move to say goodbye.

Then we're on the move, past the protesters yelling we're enabling the flesh-sins of devils, into the guard room to be strip-searched. My precious contraband of code and copper burns under my tongue's biohacked pocket.

It's all happening too fast, enough to make my head spin.

March's informant leads the way to the feeding bay. Per protocol, a second, surly guard accompanies us. I sense the worry emanating in bitter curlicues from Eden's pores. March must have a plan to distract the second guard, enough for Eden to slip into the feeding bay and me to infiltrate the lab for the first time since our mission started. March always has a plan.

A high-pitched scream resounds across gray walls, followed by a guttural growl—call and response. The second guard, alert, reaches for his weapon.

"Stay with the eating vessels," he orders March's man and sprints down the corridor with what sounds like most of the facility's personnel.

"Who was that?" I ask. My marrow chills and jellies with some fear I cannot place. "That voice, the first one. Didn't it sound familiar?"

Before Eden can reply, March's man shakes his head while red lights flare overhead.

"Hacker girl, run to the lab, now. You know the way—I risked my neck to get you the blueprints. You have a minute before guard change while we deal with the emergency protocol."

I still don't know what March's distraction entailed. With one last look at Eden, I dash through Kratos on sound-absorbing boots. My breath mists the stale air. My modified jumpsuit repels camera lenses, swathing my silhouette under a blank veil in the footage. The lab door is unlocked, as March had promised during last night's debriefing. I steal inside the cavernous room and gape at a vista of sterilized needles, steel implements, gurneys, and tethers.

I was calm this morning, comforted by my sense of purpose acquired in the two months since Eden and I reunited. Yet now I am unsettled. The high-pitched scream, eerily familiar, taunts my ears. I survey the lab with all its machines and strange medical equipment. I picture my sister's organic material forcefully extracted to be studied and exploited by Kratos' scientists.

Doubling over, I retch. Inhale, exhale. I picture Eden in the feeding bay, talking to the Eaters in honey-soothing tones. I reach my gloved hand into my mouth, retrieve the centipede sprayed in a DNA-nullifying coat.

I spent years creating my copper-wire robot: a distraction from absent parents and my confusing lack of romantic attraction. All my fears of being unlovable were poured into that little machine.

And now, it will extract everything the lab computers have to hide—anything that the scientists have held back to serve the city's anti-Quickening agenda.

The servers whir behind a glass case at the back of the lab, past the operating tables and the hoses to wash away all the blood. Past the quarantine areas zippered close and empty. I follow my slithering centipede, which contorts its many segments small enough to slip through the cracks. The centipede needs approximately three minutes to download a perfect copy of the hard drives, then vanish without a trace. I pace, thinking I hear the phantom clinks of sharp implements, the whimpers swallowed behind gags.

The scrape of the lab door opening.

"You! What are you doing here?" It's another guard, one I've never seen before.

Panic engorges my tongue, the muscle choking me like a gobbet of meat that refuses to go down. I point to my crimson ribbon and stammer, "Nothing! I got turned around!" trying to sound dazed, high off the regeneration endorphins.

The guard approaches, one hand on his gun, the other rubbing his mouth. Appraising.

"Pretty red thing like you, all lost?" He presses into my space, making me retreat against a gurney. Metal clangs as my back slams against it. This is a sound that echoes, that haunts.

I have this image of being strapped to the gurney, wheeled into the cells of Kratos, locked behind unbreakable glass. No one will know what happened to me. Eden and Evi will wonder at first, but eventually, they will move on without me.

I struggle to focus on the guard's words as I float through undertows of panic. He can't be much older than me. One of the youths that escaped the Quickening unchanged, then. Perhaps those who thought themselves special for it.

"Hey, Red. What if I cut you up a little? Would you heal right away? Can I see?"

I gather air to scream, but alerting the whole guard would mean getting caught for good. Here, I can bargain. Grant him the red spill he craves. I force my muscles to unwind, pliant against the gurney. The guard sees and smirks.

I dredge up a giggle. Pray that my centipede— burrowed deep in data—makes it back to March unscathed.

"You'll let me do anything, won't you? Like those cannibals do. You keep coming back for more, so you must enjoy getting hurt." So, you deserve to, goes unspoken.

I bristle for Eden and the rest of the Healers. Does this foolish guard want chaos? For Eaters to go starved and wild? For Kronos to put us all down like animals? Inside me roils dread and my atoms' prolonged scream at the prospect of unwanted touch.

"Nora." Eden's voice at the door, then rushing to my side.

"I'm so sorry, mister, my friend wandered off. You know how blood loss is…. We've been working too many night shifts."

While Eden rambles, the guard backs away—a coward now that he has an audience whose gender he cannot determine at a glance.

"This is a red alert." The guard stares furrow-browed between us. "An Eater has attacked one of the guards. You can't be here, so go home already. You're clearly not in it for the money."

He watches us leave with a hand on his stun gun and the look of a starving stray.

The centipede! Eden squeezes my hand and casts their eyes subtly downward. I slacken with relief when I notice the centipede clinging to the leg cuff of my overalls. The little copper thing has known my body heat for nearly a decade—of course, it followed me with our data-extracted loot.

By the time we make it outside, I feel about to faint.

Eden hauls me toward the nearest park bench despite their own blood-loss-sway.

"I got it," I pant. "I got everything."

Eden knows better than to ask if I'm okay.

Instead, they say, "That red alert—the kid that attacked the guard? It was Ananias from our first feeding session."

I HAVE NO memory of making it home. March must have sent a cab for us—or she didn't. Eden and I stumble into the apartment my parents abandoned, and there Evi and March await, sitting apart on the couch like strangers.

"The centipede," March demands, old-fashioned laptop open and ready to receive the intel I gathered.

"The kid," I gasp, leaning against Eden. "Was it you? Did you make Ananias attack the guard?"

March's hand wavers as the centipede refuses to materialize in her open palm.

"My informant offered him money, but he didn't want it for himself. So, I transferred the creds to his sister, and Ananias agreed to distract the guards and help you complete the mission."

"You doomed him," I spit out, bridling at March's dismissiveness. "He's a kid; an Eater like us. What do you think they'll do to him in Kratos now that he's hurt a guard?"

I'm trembling against Eden, not knowing where my skin ends and theirs begins. The tentacles of our jellyfish mods entangle in terror.

I remember talking with Ananias in that depressing little room. His favorite videogames, the foods he misses most, all the many, minute secrets he shared with me. Did he think that, by giving the money to the sister who refused to visit him, she would finally forgive him for transforming during the Quickening?

Evi scoots closer to March, sliding an arm around her waist. This is the first time I've seen them touch. March tenses, a strange palsy to her jaw muscles. "We must all make sacrifices," my sister says, staring me straight in the eye. "Isn't that right, Nora?"

Red-hot and humiliated by her implication, I break eye contact. I hand the centipede to March, who lets it crawl into her laptop, as outdated as her clothing, house, and mannerisms.

My body slumps on the couch. Eden hovers, fretting and flitting from my side to March's, reading over her shoulder. March, unblinking, untiring, opens file after file to devour their contents. My mind feels slow as the wax-drip of votive candles from the apartment's altar, fast as a skipped holo-ad. Until March makes a choked-off sound akin to a malfunctioning engine. Phrases reach me fragmented through my haze...

... latent gene prevalent in all third-generation Kronos citizens... trigger unknown... environmental factors undetermined.

Not a virus, then. We've always known the Quickening had never been contagious. That the scientists had lied to us. According to Kratos' files, the so-called vaccine was just a temporary gene suppressant while more experiments were secretly conducted on the unQuickened population. The Quickened gene had pre-existed in my entire generation antepartum. Upon activation, it changed Eater and Healer anatomies from within in opposite but complementary directions. Nature does not do things by halves, even at the end—and beginning—of the world. The new hunger, and the new satiation, evolved hand-in-hand through natural selection.

Kronos whelped every one of its children this way, then blamed them for the first wave of transformations. Claimed we caused it by hacking our bodies, minds, DNA. It was only a matter of chance whose gene was activated. Only a matter of time who Quickened first but never last.

The truth, at last, was revealed: the city couldn't kill every last of its latent-gene children, so Kronos and the rest of the cluster cities imprisoned only the known troublemakers, hoping the fear would keep the rest from Quickening.

I glean all this through rapid conversation penetrating the treacly substance of my mind. Through a vast and yawning chasm, I become aware of Eden by my side, gently shaking my shoulder. Evi hugs March, whose arms hang limp, unwilling or unable to return the embrace.

From my vantage point, I can see March's eyes, burning and bottomless. A new hunger I cannot put into words.

PART III
CARNIVALE
CANNIBALE

EDEN AND I slept for a long time. Every few hours, we jolt awake, soothing ourselves and each other over and over like a broken algorithm.

My hands feel dirty, used. Sounds echo: Ananias' screams, Evi's whimpers—is she strapped to a gurney or crying through night terrors? Am I? I taste smoke and ash and copper as my centipede—despite all evidence being eradicated leg by self-cannibalized leg—dream-crawls inside my orifices. The young guard taunts me, touches me. Pretty red, pretty red.

The next time we awaken, Eden whispers, "When Ananias fed from me, all his projected thoughts were about making it back home and being forgiven."

Tomorrow are the mayoral elections, when March will release the genome sequence to the public. The

Kronos officials will be painted as enablers of deception and scapegoating, muddling the cluster-cities' culpability in our evolution. Chaos will foment through every molecule under Kronos' dome, until unrest fogs the glass prison that contains us.

"I've been thinking..." Eden says. "We ruined this planet. Depleted all resources, made the atmosphere unlivable. What if the Quickening was just evolution's way of preparing us for some new catastrophe down the line?"

I think about butterflies changing wing shapes and colors between generations to avoid extinction. Maybe we were indeed nature's prototypes, like another Gaia and Ouranos. And perhaps the violence and unpredictability of the Quickening means something went wrong with our evolutions, distorting our new half-cooked era of symbiosis. All I can think of is our catastrophe, city-wide and cupped between our palms. The broken glass and charred remains, the black vans and silver gurneys, the child martyrs and unquiet youth.

I drown my bitter laughter into the skin of Eden's neck. The house is quiet, but for the hum of my devices and the security system I installed. Evi must have left with March, perhaps to plan another lavish party celebrating today's revelations.

I don't know who moves first, but Eden and I are touching, desperate for proof we are not dead. Reaching between their legs, I cup their hardness in my palm, then let their soft curves slot against me, breast to breast. Eden whimpers sweetly against my ear as my grip tightens around them, working them as swiftly as I know they like. I feel no such vibration, only a vicarious hunger for more. I think about what we learned about our genes. And earlier still, how I once worried that, even in the age of sexual freedom, my body and mind were faulty mechanisms. But we are whole, Eden and I. The parts of us that are contradictory and complementary, and everything in between.

Me asking is this good, are you close, you feel so alive, I want you this alive always. And Eden, baring their neck to me, guiding my predator's mouth to their rabbiting pulse—an offering of flesh. I clutch and cradle, are you certain, do you remember your safeword from when I used to tie you up, toy with you, fuck you slow? Do you know how to stop me if it gets too much?

Eden nodding, gods, please. I've always rejoiced in taking them apart and now is no different. Eden's jellyfish tattoo undulates like a pulse, tentacles tickling my lips, drawing me in. My teeth do their hungry work worshipping at their skin and the scars I gave them. A new palimpsest of trauma rewritten and preserved.

I bite down. Tendons strain under the skin, the muscle rippling minutely with each moan. My tooth enamel meeting bone is an electrifying sensation. The meat-offering slides like a caress down my throat. Eden's taste fulminates through my gums and palate, starbursting to each last nerve ending.

This willing consumption may be the last step toward mending our broken bond.

In the aftermath, we hold each other. Eden's eyelashes are pearled with tears. They always cried during sex, a reflex of repressed emotion born from years of foster families deeming them too high maintenance. No wonder they're so good at feeding those in need. Yet it's my turn now to care for them. To contain the flux of feelings pouring through our feeding bond. My tongue dutifully cleans the blood pooling in the juncture between their neck and shoulder. When we kiss, we taste each other's memories. And we taste each other.

"It's time to leave," I breathe into Eden. "Kronos has gotten too dangerous for us."

"What about our mission?" Eden asks.

"We can still help long-distance. Build new ties in whatever sibling-city Polydor@'s people place us in." Mnemosyne, maybe, where the Quickened were released from quarantine early and bloodlessly. Or Iapetos—the city officials offer special amnesty for Eater/Healer pairs moving in together.

Geographical mobility is increasingly onerous between sibling-cities, and impossible between different clusters. We only see the newer domes—the Olympians to our Titans—on our holo-screens. More verdant, more vibrant, more technologically advanced than our gray streets could ever dream of. I am unregistered, while Eden is considered dead in Kronos' records. Nobody will look for us if something goes wrong and we're detained crossing cities. But still, we must try.

Eden hesitates. I brush the sweat-matted curls away from their eyes. The skin of their eyelids is velvet-soft against the whorls of my thumb. "But you like it here," they say. "You found your purpose, your people."

"You are my people," I seethe, to make them believe me.

"And Evi?"

I think about my sister's heartfelt, heartbreaking expression on so many placards and holo-screens—the face of the revolution. And underneath, the crippling loneliness. The daily Psychopomp IVs. Something has been broken between me and Evi. A porcelain piece shattered into manifold sisterly parts, and I did not know the code to fix it.

"Evi will forgive me," I say. "She has her girlfriend, her media campaign, her fans. I'm only holding her back."

Eden doesn't call out my lie. How, for them, I will become a coward anew.

I WATCH EVI sleep in the silver-tinged dark.

When she was gone, I compulsively checked my holo-screen every minute. I forced myself to sleep light enough to hear her come home in the middle of the night. I was so certain she'd escape. She was Evi, and you do not lock Evi up or force her to act against her will. My sister would come back to me and tell me it was okay. She was not mad; she was here now.

But I haven't been here in weeks, not in spirit. I watch my sister as if through Palimpsest's layers. How she was: my protector and only confidante, the one I wanted to spend my life with, in a fairytale castle all by ourselves. And as she is now: petty and manipulative, sad and angry, holding tooth and nail to some fragile, fragmented hope.

My sister. Always my brilliant sister. And I'm about to abandon her like our parents did to us both. We're a little bit sick, Evi and I. We hide things in the rotten cavities of our chests, and we never say sorry or goodbye where the other can hear.

I tuck the blankets around Evi's dream-sweating form and kiss the salt on her brow. I know I have not settled my debt to her. Debts like ours can never be repaid.

I take only a pack of clothes and some of my devices, mourning the ones I leave behind. March can give them to my replacement. Or Evi will throw them away like she accused me of doing with her belongings. I pray our forged papers—another one of Polydor@'s many gifts—will hold through the excruciating bureaucracy of moving between cluster-cities. The travel restrictions and steep ticket prices—surveillance masquerading as sustainability.

"Bye-bye, for now, Evi," I say, a little kid again.

Eden has picked up their leftover belongings from March's mansion. We will set things right with March and leave Eden and me together. Polydor@ has agreed to let us crash at eir and Nikolas' place until it's safe to cross cities. I don't order a cab this time, nor do I use Palimpsest. I only walk through the streets of Kronos, the city that eats and spits out its young, absorbing all its wretched, resplendent glory under the rising dawn.

I am going to tell March that I'm done, ask her to take care of my sister, and perhaps even give Eden and me her blessing. Jonah March may be many things, but she was still the orchestrator of our revolution, even if I cannot reconcile my budding affinity for her with the dubious things she's done.

And if I leave a part of my heart with Evi—a big, red chunk of myself beating for my sister alone—she is free to squash it underfoot or cradle it in her hand until we meet again.

THE MANSION IS eerily quiet, devoid of thumping music or sleeping partygoers. No Crimson Ribbons coming in after a night of work, either. I let myself in through the back entrance, treading familiar paths. Glitter and debris litter the kitchen, front room, and ballroom like nobody has bothered to clean in days. I cannot suppress my shudder on the way upstairs. Perhaps this is my cowardice returning after months of swallowing it down.

March is always up before dawn, never genuinely allowing herself to rest. The door to the study stands ajar, amber light streaming from within. Before I can knock, a banging sound stills me. My hairs prickle to attention. It keeps coming, this horrible sound, like something soft and giving, meeting a hard surface repeatedly. I want to announce myself, but now that I'm nearly at the door, I can hear March's distorted voice. Her words—usually so perfectly enunciated—all slur together into a mantra.

It takes me a moment to realize what she's repeating in time to the fleshy-wet thuds: the Unquiet Quicken first.

I can't stand it anymore. I enter March's study to find her standing before her full-length mirror. Her suit is wrinkled, her tie undone, and her hair disheveled for the first time since I've met her. An ugly gash mars her forehead, where she's been banging her head against the mirror's thick brass frame as she repeated Kronos' favorite propagandas to her reflection.

The Unquiet Quicken first. Cursed are the Eaters. UnquietEatersQuickenCursed.

I don't know what I'm seeing. What I've stumbled into unannounced. "March...."

A gut-sunk instinct inside me—not a predator's, but a prey's—wants to send me running for the door, never mind the bag I've dropped on the floor or what I came here to tell March. Just flee from whatever this is, find Eden, and get out.

Then, March faces away from the mirror. Toward me. Blood trickles down like ruby teardrops between her eyes, yet her gaze burns me, candescent coals pinning me in place.

"Nora," March says in a broken voice—a not-March voice. I'm so glad someone came." Her usual composure is cracked down the middle. Her familiar constraint and economy, a vanishing act. This is March, unraveled.

Before I can say anything, she lurches around me and locks the study door. I picture Eden elsewhere in the mansion, and I can't tell if I'm relieved they won't witness whatever's happening here or scared I am now locked alone with a mercurial March. The key disappears into the inner pocket of her suit jacket. Nobody uses analog keys anymore. Curse this whole antiquated mansion, completely unhackable.

"March... Jonah, is everything okay?"

What a useless question. There's nothing okay about this. She's pacing the office like a caged animal in its enclosure, and I am a visitor trapped here with her hunger.

"I've been good, haven't I?" March says, though I don't think it's me she's addressing. She sways back to the mirror that bears her blood. Through her reflection, we watch each other. "Always so perfect. Good grades, good morals, made my parents proud, unlike the rest of my unquiet generation. Never got any body mods except for the smallest tattoo—and oh, I paid for that dearly in front of my parents' entire congregation."

Should I step forward or back? Comfort March or let her finish her terrible monologue sending frissons of fear along my synapses?

"So why was I chosen to be an Eater? Why was I transformed during the Quickening? A mistake, Nora. Can't you see it was all a mistake, and I was the one chosen to correct it from the inside?"

Three things occur to me at once. Jonah March is drunk. Jonah March hates herself. Jonah March is not who she's claimed to be.

"Corrected," I stammer, chilled to the bone. "How?"

I remember the Kratos laboratory, the data March wanted my copperwire centipede to steal for her, and the genome sequence she said would reveal the truth about our people, sparing us from the mayor's death-sentence dome.

My mind whirs like one of my robotic creations, yet it feels like the flyaway threads of reason and meaning are impossible for me to seize into coherence. "The lab findings. You wanted to—said you wanted to release everything to the public. Influence the elections in our favor. That's why you needed my centipede, right?" I shout the last word, though I know from previous visits that the study walls are soundproof. We are locked in a deprivation chamber, March and I. And she laughs and laughs, her lilting voice transmuting into a gravelly rasp. A sound as terrible as Ananias' scream in Kratos when I doomed him to his ruin.

"Find the genome, isolate it, and eliminate it," March replies, as aloofly as if discussing Kronos' lab-controlled weather. "Every child, teenager, and young adult under the dome is already a lost cause. But we could save future generations from another monstering while quarantining ourselves under a new dome. Your findings helped. I must thank you."

"Eliminate," I say, unable to catch my breath. "That sounds an awful lot like eugenics."

March never wanted to rehabilitate the public image of the Quickened or expose the facilities' lies to the public. She didn't want us to prove that the Quickening had never been a sickness or a personal failing but the all-encompassing will of nature, biology, and evolution.

She just wanted us dead, wanted us gone, paying the price for the crimes of progenitors past.

"You have to understand, Nora," she says, laughter or sobs wracking her body, blood spurting from her wound. "We are monsters, all of us, Eaters and Healers. My parents' religion predicted this would happen if we abandoned natural living, biohacked our bodies, overused technology. Stray from the path of righteousness, and you'll have little kids monstering next. What if the whole unquiet world sprouts teeth and eats itself to the quick?"

She chants again and laughs, laughs and chants, the Unquiet Quicken first.

March's perfect façade, broken. Her perfect clothes wrinkled. Her perfect hair unslicked. Her perfect plan, nothing but a labyrinthine betrayal.

March killed her parents, yet she still repeats their words of abuse like a creed above the lives of all of Kronos' segments and strata.

"You used us," I say through a mouthful of bitter spit. "Used me."

March's voice blisters with disgust. "Your sister would never have seen things my way. But you're smart. You know we must stop this illness of genes and morality from spreading." Blood plasters her hair against her skull. With every step she takes toward me, I take one back.

"It's too late for me to save Kronos now. But others will continue what I started."

More bitter realizations flood my system. We were each unknowingly called to play a different game. A different ruse. Her media campaign to make us palatable to Kronos' citizens distracted Evi, while March fed Evi's anger and the need to be loved. Eden's firm caring streak was exploited to gain entry into Kratos. My guilt and aimless lack of belonging was manipulated after Evi blabbered about my centipede in Kratos, and March coveted my copperwire data thief for her own twisted cause.

A revolution that Jonah March had never planned to undergo. An artificial liberation delivered to the Quickened of Kronos.

And now I am trapped here with her.

I run to the locked door and bang my palms against the heavy oak, hoping someone, anyone, comes. Teeth against my throat, a fevered weight down my back. Mach groans as she bites off a piece of my shoulder to stop me from escaping and exposing her. Or perhaps just to punish me, punish us both. Her tightly coiled hunger is finally coming unrepressed, running loose. With my mass of meat in March's mouth, I scream at the burn of broken skin and pierced muscle, ripped tendons, and flowing blood. But more than that, I bridle at the hubris—the taboo—the violation—of an Eater partaking unnegotiated of another.

I push March away from me as I slide against the door. March does not resist me. She looks as violated as I feel, but it brings me no joy—only anger. I remember Eden's description of March during feedings: aloof, self-hating, dissociating. And how March flinched from my touch at the pre-electoral rally, as if fearing corruption and contagion—Kronos' propaganda running deep even among those already Quickened.

"Jonah," I say, hand pressed to my wound, slippery with my own lifeforce. "Whatever they told you, whatever you think you're doing here, you must stop."

She only shakes her head. Wiping her sleeve across the blood on her face, she stumbles back to her desk. She might be crying. Warily, I watch her grab an injection from one of the drawers—the syringe glitters Psychopomp-pink. The second object she shakily retrieves looks like a silver lighter, heavy and engraved. Upon thrusting the needle into her arm, March's countenance shifts. What does she see? A new world of no hunger and satiation—no Eater and Healer symbiotes? The traditional life her dead parents dreamed for her? Or is it her own personal heaven slipping through the cracks, somewhere far from her parents' leashes and the terrible legacy they bequeathed her?

No matter. Whatever Psychopomp is showing March bolsters her determination and makes it easier for her to do what she thinks is necessary.

Gaunt and ghoulish, Jonah March picks up the lighter. Her eyes stare off into the Psychopomp void. And still, she resembles a little lost kid, beaten down and told she was wrong her entire life, told to be good or else. Until she unquieted during the Quickening, monstering like her family had always warned her about.

"I'm not sorry to kill my kind," March says, stained with her blood and mine. The hunger, at last, has gone out of her eyes. As if they are already dead. She hesitates before looking at me. What she did to me. "I'm only sorry this had to be you."

That's when March uncaps the silver lighter—the incendiary device—and—

She self-immolates.

THE FIRE SPREADS swiftly. First, it swallows March into a flame pillar and screams, blackened pain. Then, a hungering beast, the fire eats away at the study: the gilded mirror, the carved desk, the green leather chairs. In the pomegranate still life, red arils burst open like blood vessels. The extravagant displays of wealth and antiquity—her family's conservative visions—all go up in flames. Even as plumes of smoke choke my lungs, dazzling me in conjunction with the blood loss, the part of me born and raised in Kronos expects the smoke sensors to blare to life and the fire-brigade bots to swarm the house as per security protocols. Even, perhaps, for the flames to be extinguished alone.

Nothing happens.

I wrench my eyes away from the burning husk—the howling, self-made martyr—that is March. I run to the door, yelping as the embossed brass knob burns my palm. It leaves an engraving of roses bubbling away on my skin while the fire turns everything around me red-hot and suffocating.

It's spreading lower too, an igneous dissemination across the mansion. Eden is in here somewhere, waiting for us to begin our new lives far from all-devouring Kronos. It's what we always promised to each other. We will grow old together. We will....

But the lock won't open. The fire refuses to devour itself to nothing. I kick at the door frame, but the wood is opulently thick. The only physical key is in the suit pocket of March, who has by now crumbled behind her desk, a poor monster burning out of sight. Her charred skin still assaults my nostrils.

I don't know who else remains in this mansion. How many Eaters and Healers, rebels and revelers? March had turned this place into a so-called haven for all. Yet her immolation has doomed me, Eden, and everyone else.

A winged memory slices through my haze—meeting

Eden here for the first time post-Quickening. I glance at the scorched floral panels of the folding screen, the paper curling in on itself. Through the smoking gaps peeks the door to the utility corridor. I fly through the flames, heedless of how they singe my skin and clothing. I bite out bloody prayers to gods and giants that the doorway is unlocked; that me catching March by surprise equals one last chance at escape. Find Eden and get out of here, get out, get out, get out.

I possess no recollection of having run through the utility corridor and out the kitchen exit. Next, I am aware, I'm rolling in the grass hemmed in by towering hedges as I strive to put out the fire of me. My hair smells like riots and burnt debris, and half of my scalp feels molten and misshapen. The wound March gouged into me still gapes open. Regeneration hums in unfocused bursts, reminiscent of when I devoured Eden during the Quickening, and it took them such a long time to recover. The scars my hunger left behind never fully healed.

I have no illusions I will come out of this without new scar clusters of my own.

Eden! Memory sparks me to horrid wakefulness. I try to climb to my feet, stumbling, falling back into the sooty grass—I need to find Eden. But March's mansion is up in flames, the dawn-dark sky engulfed by a new hunger rising ashen and all-encompassing toward Kronos' dome.

I stare around me with eyes squinted, half-closed. Through the choking smoke, I see no other soul on the lawn. I circle the house, but the windows are walled off by amber-burnished flames, and the front door's awning has collapsed, with marble pillars slumped into a cross-shape. Antique and ancient and disregarding safety regulations—the past burns.

Eden knew about the secret passageway. Did they escape the fire like I did, hiding somewhere off March's estate to avoid being questioned and arrested once the police arrived? Or, what if they ran up to March's study through the fire, looking for me? What if my best friend is trapped under a burning beam or fallen down the stairs, regeneration unable to keep up with the raging inferno?

The blood trickling down my body and the smoke trapped under Kronos' dome cloud my thinking. Eden is smart. Eden said we would run away together, and this is what we shall do.

Sirens sound in the distance through my tinnitus-ringing ears. I half-run, half-hobble down the rose-strewn garden path toward the street. An unregistered Eater on the scene of the crime will only raise more suspicions. I need to hide. I need to find Eden. My holo-screen got damaged in the fire—it cannot access Palimpsest and find a safe space nearby. I run down several twisting side streets toward town, the mansions and maisonettes of the rich giving way to towering skyscrapers and steel-dressed shopping establishments.

Then, the shriek of sirens is swallowed by the sound of music and chants. In the throes of blazing chaos, I had forgotten today dawns the morning of the mayoral elections.

A party or protest pours inexorable down the street.

IN THE MASKED parade, birds of paradise caw their glittering anger. Faces swim into my blurring vision, but I can't tell if they're covered in fake feathers or if the bruise-purple plumage is modified to grow from their pores. Dazed, I run through the crowd from opposite directions, like stroking the fur of a cat's back wrong.

Wrong, it's all wrong, isn't it?

"Eden!" I scream myself raw, trying to find them through the wilding crowd while behind me, March's mansion burns. "Please!"

Once Eden is here, everything will be made right again. We're just playing hide-and-seek. Yes. Eden is waiting for me to find them, as I failed to do after the Quickening.

People jostle my open wound, their faces distorted behind carnival masks. Some try to touch my burned flesh—my gaping meat—thinking it a mod, a costume. My unquiet generation dances through the streets, chanting condemnations of injustice, feeding freely on each other. Oneiric flashes reach me: the beaks of plague doctor masks, the dirty lace of flowing gowns, the rictus smiles of red-lipped revelers.

I catch a flash of my sister's face in the crowd, but it's only a placard. The used martyr, the face of the revolution—Evi, whom I left back home sleeping in blessed Psychopomp oblivion. I want the sister I abandoned to come and take the blame for me. Tell me she's been hiding Eden from me again. She is sorry, but she will give them back now.

I never told Eden I'm sorry.

I yell their name through smoke-abused lungs. My vision turns red with the memory of flames imprinting danger behind my retinas. I don't need Palimpsest for my city to glow the red of blood. "Eden, where are you?"

The crowd screams, too, thinking my grief a protest call. A palimpsest, me and my people I ran from, the people I tried to help, the people I unknowingly betrayed. The rapid drumbeat matches my pulse. A party or a funeral procession? A crimson ribbon twists through the parade. I follow it, thinking it belongs to Eden, a red string of fate connecting us. Broken bottles shine like fallen stars on the tarmac under my unsteady feet. Except, should the stars fall, they will only splatter and stain the city's glass convex. Red as the bloodied hands of Kronos.

Among the glittering, fuming crowd, my hunger and I chase our own tails.

And the crowd thrums with a ravening that recognizes mine. A tune for, if not reformation, then ruination. The fall of the dome upon us all. Fuck their gods, fuck their giants. Let Kronos fly apart at the seams in a rain of glass, guts, and glitter. Let their miracle city devour itself.

I push deeper through the revelers. The crowd's hunger swallows me whole.

ABOUT THE AUTHOR

Avra Margariti is a queer author, Greek sea
monster,and Rhysling-nominated poet with a
fondness for the dark and the darling. Avra's
work haunts publications such as *Strange Horizons*,
Apex, *The Deadlands*, *Asimov's*, *F&SF*, *Podcastle*,
and elsewhere.

You can find Avra on twitter & bluesky
@avramargariti